Under the Mistletoe:

Love from a Hood Pharmacist

TN Jones

Under the Mistletoe: Love from a Hood Pharmacist
Copyright © 2020 by TN Jones.

This book is a work of fiction. Names, characters, places, and incidents either are products of the author's imagination or are used fictitiously. Any resemblance to actual persons, living or dead, events, or locales is entirely coincidental.

Acknowledgment

First, thanks must go out to the Higher Being for providing me with a sound body and mind, in addition to having the natural talent of writing and blessing me with the ability to tap into such an amazing part of life.

Second, thanks most definitely go to my Prin Pretty; you mean the world to me. Without you, I wouldn't be anything. Mommy loves you, yes, I do!

Third, to my lovely readers and supporters who have been rocking with me since day one.

Fourth, to the lovely new readers for giving me a chance.

Like always, I wouldn't have made it this far without anyone. I genuinely thank everyone for staying ten toes down with me, no matter what I drop. Muah! Y'all make this writing journey enjoyable and have once again trusted me to provide all of you with quality entertainment.

Chapter One

NaTashia Robertson

Thanksgiving 2019

As I looked around my mother's crowded house, I didn't feel pleasant about being around a few family members and plenty of friends of the family. I wanted to be left alone. However, the mighty Glorianna Jean Robertson wouldn't have anyone living under her roof missing on one of the most celebrated holidays of the year.

I couldn't be merry or have a smile on my face. I had problems that needed to be handled. I had to figure out what I was going to do. Mostly, how I would heal mentally from the newfound news of my recently deceased lover, Joseph Minnow, and his asshole of a family. I needed to comprehend how I didn't see the signs of him being a married man with children outside of the two children I bore for him. Badly, I needed to know how his family could disclaim my children and why he didn't leave us anything. Amongst those things, I had to wrap my head around being in my home state, raising my children in peace without my mother down my fucking neck.

"Hey, cousin. Why are you sitting over here looking lost?" Sharee inquired as she sat next to me, scooping a small serving of potato salad on the plastic spoon.

"Because I am."

"Everyone falls on their ass at least once in their lives, NaTashia. It's nothing to be ashamed of. You will bounce back in no time. I know Auntie Glorianna can be a handful, but try not to let her beat you down. Just take a deep breath and talk to her. She'll understand you."

Shaking my head, I tried to keep the tears from streaming down my face as I said, "I don't think she will ever understand me. She won't stop talking long enough to hear a single word out of my mouth. All she knows is to rant and rave with a dash of belittling. It's been that way since I was born. Either it's do shit her way and do it promptly, or I can do it her way, and she's still pissed."

With a raised eyebrow, Sharee glared at me and said, "Pray about it. It will get better. I promise."

Nodding, I nonchalantly said, "Okay."

As more people filled into my mother's decorative home, I zoned out and thought about the day my life changed, a week ago.

I was sitting on the sofa, folding clothes. My beautiful children were outside playing. A few knocks sounded on the screen door, resulting in me hopping to my feet with a smile on my face. I welcomed the stranger of a pretty, average height, and fair-skinned woman into my home. The look on her face wasn't a pleasant one. Her posture was outstanding—zero slouching. By the expression on her face, I could tell she was intimidated by me, but I didn't understand why. After taking a seat, I informed the woman she should do so. She refused.

Confused by her stance, I stood and asked, "Who are you, and how may I help you?"

"I'm Joseph Minnow's wife, Liddia. I found these papers hidden well in the cupboard of my husband's work office. That's how I learned of you, your children with my husband, the car, and this nice house, which is two hours away from the home my husband and I share," she firmly voiced, glaring into my face.

The air was knocked out of me as my knees buckled. I wanted to make sure I heard her correctly; therefore, I said, "Come again?"

"You heard me well. Now, I have some questions for you since he can't answer any of them," she spoke through clenched teeth, top lip curled upward.

With a rapidly racing heart, I asked, "Why can't he answer them? He should be the one you talk to, not me? For the record, I never knew he was married."

"Tuh," she chuckled sinisterly before continuing, "You women always claim you didn't know. I'm sure there were signs he was married. You just didn't pay attention. Anyways, he can't answer any of my questions because he's dead."

At the same time, I cupped my mouth and dropped to the ground. I closed my eyes and prayed I was dreaming. Joseph was supposed to have arrived at the airport today at five o'clock p.m. I was to pick him up.

"Anyways, I didn't come by here on a friendly note. I'm here on behalf of his family. You are not to show face at his funeral. They will not claim the children he has with you. You are not in his will.

Outside of social security, neither you nor your children will receive anything. *Since your name isn't on the deed of this house, you and your children will* have to leave. You have six days to exit this place. The car you drive, which is in his name, I will be taking it."

"Family? Joseph told me he was estranged from his family," I shrieked, tears cascading down my dark-chocolate face.

Shaking her head, Liddia replied, "Classic, cheating husband's words; yet, you believed him."

""He gave me no reason not to believe him."

With much attitude, Liddia glared at me nastily and said, "Well, now you know firsthand, he wasn't estranged. Once a week, we had family dinners with his parents."

I couldn't believe any of the things I'd heard. Not only was my lover dead, but everything he told me was a lie. I had been living a lie for years without any indication. I felt so stupid.

While Liddia reiterated that my children and I would leave our home with nothing, I was beyond hurt and stunned.

Slowly rising off the floor, I walked towards the sofa and replied, "What am I going to do?"

"I don't know, and I really don't care," Liddia nastily voiced.

Feeling as if I was in the twilight zone, I stared at the ground. My mind seemed as if it was inside of a tornado. My heart felt as if it was in the middle of a volcano. My body seemed as if it was shaken by the most violent earthquake the earth had ever experienced.

Sighing deeply, Liddia asked, "Where are the car keys?"

I pointed towards the kitchen and said, "On the key rack beside the refrigerator."

As she stomped towards the kitchen, she mumbled something. I didn't care to know what she had said. My world had shifted underneath my feet. I did the one thing I swore I would never do: put my trust in a man. I did the stupidest thing ever: I didn't return to work after having our second child. I became the nurturer while Joseph provided. I did the craziest thing ever: I didn't press him to put my name on the house or car. I was never the careless type. How could I have been so reckless with him?

Standing inches away from me, Liddia asked, sniffling, "Did you love him?"

Angrily, I stood and shouted, "I gave him two fucking kids! I gave up my life because he asked me to! I became the very person I vowed never to be because of him! So, what the fuck do you think, Liddia?"

"Did you really not know he was married?"

Honestly, I replied, "No, I didn't."

"How long have you and Joseph been dealing with each other?"

Becoming sassy, I replied, "If you know about my children, then you know how long Joseph and I have been together. But since you want to be an asshole, I will tell you. We have an eight-year-old daughter and a ten-year-old son."

As tears welled in her eyes, I wiped mine off my rounded face and pointed towards the door. There wasn't anything left to say. She nodded and stepped away from me.

Placing her hand on the screen door, Liddia looked at me and wholeheartedly said, "I guess I should tell you ... I'm sorry for your loss because he surely wasn't a loss to our ten-year-old son and me. He was barely home. Always said he was on a business trip. Now, I guess you and his little family were 'the business trip'. You have six days to get out of this house before I send someone in here to clear this motherfucker out."

And just like that, my life did a three-sixty turn.

"We in hereee!" my uncle, who was more like a brother to me, shouted, snapping me into reality.

Behind him were his best friends from our adolescent years: Fabien and June Bug. Each one held a case of drinks and beer. All were higher than a dinosaur's ass. Each one had swag like none other; yet, they weren't the settling down type. Those three niggas were certified drug dealing whores.

"Look at my niecey-pooh. I'm so glad you are back in town. It's been dull as hell without you." Cleophus smiled as I stood.

Lightly smiling, I strolled towards my uncle, all the while speaking to his beloved crew. In the proximity of my five-foot-eleven uncle, we engaged in a tight embrace.

Whispering in my ear, "You know my sister told me what happened. I will flatline that nigga's whole line. Give me the word an' I'mma make that shit happen soon as I finish eatin'."

Glaring into his handsome face, I replied, "That's not necessary."

Lowly, he replied, "Shid, in my eyes, it is. I don't like anyone denyin' my fam. You know how I feel 'bout my blood an' close buddies."

Deeply inhaling, I nodded and said, "Yeah, I know, but trust me ... sit this one out. They aren't worth it."

"Cleophus!" my momma yelled, causing everyone to look our way.

"Sis, what I told you 'bout callin' my name like that," my uncle laughed.

"Boy, get your silly ass in here," Momma chuckled.

"My damn sister finna preach me out the house," he voiced, shaking his head.

"Better you than me," I replied in an unpleasant tone.

"Like always, I'll have your back. I'll chop her ass down a bit," he stated, extending his hand.

As I placed my hand into his firm hand, I replied, "If your chopping hasn't been successful yet, it won't be."

While my uncle, who was two years older than me, and June Bug strolled towards the kitchen, Cleophus' main buddy stood in front of me, gazing into my eyes. The buddy I had a small crush on ever since we reached the middle of our teenage years. The buddy I hated I had cared for with every fiber in me, but I was too frightened to tell him how I felt. Before I left Alabama, seventeen years ago, Fabian Wells was the only person I considered my best friend.

"It's good to see you, Nana," Fabian's husky voice stated as he glared into my eyes.

My current situation and my past clashed, resulting in me being one bitter and angry female.

"Hm, hm," I replied as I sauntered away.

The rest of my night went just like that—fewer words spoken and a need to be anti-social. I wasn't feeling this family gathering. Nothing was right in my world. My family and their friends were the last people on earth I wanted to be around. I escaped the hell hole for a reason.

All I wanted was for everything to go back to normal: the house I had with my kids, Joseph alive, and my calm peace of mind.

Chapter Two

Fabian Wells

Upon learning my only female best friend was back in town for a while, I was elated. The day NaTashia left Alabama, she swore she would never return unless her life depended on it. For years, I hated Nana for deserting me as if I was the one who mistreated her. I hated her because she didn't stick to anything we had promised one another during our younger years. I went through so much without her; there wasn't a single time she went through shit alone.

Honestly, I thought we were in a good place and always would be.

On the low, I always had a crush on her. I believed she knew it, but she never said anything about it. Seeing her after all of these years, my feelings were ten-times stronger than before. Whatever happened for her to return to a city she vowed never to visit or move back to, it had to have been severe. Her posture, tone, and the look in her eyes informed me that she was lost and didn't know what to do. Those same eyes, I used to love looking in to, were filled with sadness. I didn't see a flicker of happiness in them. I hated seeing her in that manner. I was used to her smiling, laughing, and joking. The quiet and anti-social person who sat on the sofa was too foreign to me.

When dinner was ready, she fixed her beautiful, well-mannered children's plates. Instantly, anger consumed me. There was no doubt in my mind, Angel and Maxon weren't supposed to have been my kids. Oh, the life we would've had together--if only I had spoken up the day she left.

After she gave them their plates, NaTashia kissed them on the forehead before walking out of the back door. Once I received my plate, I wandered towards the quiet woman. I had to break her out of her shell; I had to see the light in her eyes. I couldn't stand for them to be consumed by the darkness in her life.

As I watched her get comfortable in the lounge chair, a smile crept across my face while I strolled her way. The closer I arrived in her presence, the more she sighed heavily. I was sure she was annoyed by my presence, but I didn't give a damn. If she couldn't talk to anyone, she could speak to me.

Taking a seat next to her, I said, "I've missed my best female friend."

"With the many females you dealt with, I'm sure I was replaced," she shot back.

With a raised eyebrow, I sternly spoke, "Like I said, I've missed my best female friend."

"Yeah, whatever," she nastily replied, folding her arms.

"What did I do to you, NaTashia?" I asked, glaring at her.

Looking at me, she responded, "You are in my personal space. The only reason I'm out here is that no one else was."

"I know that. Now, open up and talk to me. Tell me what's going on, and how can I help?"

Chuckling, she replied, "You want to help me?"

"Yes. I've told you if there's anything you need, don't hesitate to call me, NaTashia. Nothing has changed between us," I genuinely voiced, reaching for her hand.

Placing her hand in her lap, she gave me the nastiest glare and said, "I don't need shit from you. I'm good. Whatever I need, I'm going to get it on my own. Now, if you don't mind, please leave me the fuck alone."

While I placed the plate on the ground, I stepped to NaTashia and kneeled. Glaring into her eyes, I growled, "Don't you ever talk to me like that because I would never talk to you as if you are nothing. We used to tell each other everything, and I mean everything. You left and changed. You forgot about the one person who had your back more than Cleophus. You deserted the one person who loved you more than you would ever know. The one fucking person who would've given you the world and his last name; anyways, I don't know what happened to make you come home, but one motherfucking thing is for sure, I didn't cause you any pain. I'm not the reason you are back in your mother's house. I have never caused you any troubles or heartaches, nor will I ever. Now, if you want me gone and never inquire about you again ... say the words nicer than what you have, and I promise you ... I will never talk to you again as long as there is breath in my body. You know what, fuck that ... you don't have to say shit. You said enough already. Best of luck to you and your kids. It was a pleasure seeing you again, NaTashia."

As the wind blew harshly, I picked up the plate and walked towards the closed sliding door.

Lowly, she rambled, "I'm sorry, Fabian. I'm going through a lot right now. The man I had children with did the unthinkable. Now, I don't know what to do. I don't want to be here. I was deceived by the one I had children with. I don't like how his wife spoke to me as if I was a home wrecker. I don't like how his family chose not to be in my children's lives. I don't like how I'm perceived, and I sure as hell don't like the fact my kids' paternal family disowning them. Before you ask, no I didn't know he was married. I didn't have a single fucking clue. I left here with money in my pockets and a place of my own. I returned with nothing but clothes and my children's toys. I don't like how they stripped everything away from me as if I was the person who wronged them. They fucking crippled me, Fabian, or should I say I crippled myself. I'm never going to be able to trust a man or myself again. I'm a stupid fool to trust people, and right now I'm scared, angry, and frustrated as hell."

Turning around, I deeply inhaled. Glaring at the wet-faced, beautiful creature shaking from head to toe, I softly said, "NaTashia, you don't have to be frustrated, scared, or angry. I will always be here for you. All you have to do is open your mouth and tell me what you want. Just because you've been out of my life for close to two decades doesn't mean anything. On your fourteenth birthday, what did we promise each other?"

As I sat next to NaTashia, she slowly said, "That we would always be each other's rock."

Slowly nodding my head, I replied, "Right."

While I held her trembling, petite hand, I welcomed the wind howling as it ruffled a few strands of my beard.

Inside the house, the loud, rowdy people were having a grand time. Usually, I would be amongst them, stirring up jokes and kid-friendly chaotic noise. Yet, at the precise moment, I felt I was right where I needed to be.

"NaTashia?" I softly called out, eyes glaring at her *still* perfect slim-thick physique.

"Yeah," she responded, closing her eyes.

"I must ask this. How in the hell you didn't know the nigga was married? I was sure he gave you signs. Are you telling me you never met his family or friends?"

"There were no signs. He was always with us, except when he went on business trips. Yes, I've met his friends; well, they are his working buddies. He told me his family disowned him when he decided to not take up the family business."

"How long was he gone for business? What did he do?"

"Twice a month. The days would be different. If he was gone for four days during the week, the next time he would be gone on the weekend. He was a senior vice president of finance for a multi-billion dollar company.

Astonished, I replied, "So, y'all were out and about in the city y'all lived in and never ran into his family?"

"Nope."

"So, how in the hell did the wife know about you?"

"Papers stashed in his home office cupboard."

"Shit," I quickly voiced before saying, "NaTashia, I'm sorry you have to endure this. Do the kids know their father is dead?"

Shaking her head, she said, "No. I haven't found the will to tell them."

"Have they been asking about him?"

Nodding, she voiced, "Yes."

"What have you been telling them?"

"He's still on business and that he loves them," she replied, voice cracking.

"Damn, NaTashia. Baby girl, you need to tell them the truth. You don't have to tell them about their paternal grandparents or the wife, but you should inform them of their father's passing."

"I know. I just don't want to breakdown in front of them," she voiced as I slowly raised her hand towards my mouth.

After I placed several kisses on the back of her hand, I turned her head so she could look at me. "If you want me by your side when you do so, I will be there. If you want to have a small, private memorial for you and them, I will foot that bill. Okay?"

Before she could respond, the sliding door opened. The noise from inside grew louder outside. As we looked towards the door, I observed the tall, lanky male eyeing NaTashia with a sympathetic expression.

"Ethan, what are you doing here?" NaTashia questioned as she stood, shocked.

"I've been trying to find you ever since I learned of Joseph's death," he stated, walking towards us.

"Why?" she inquired.

The lanky individual glared at me before he placed his eyes on NaTashia. Seeing he wanted to speak with her in private, I stood and said, "I'll be inside."

Surprised at my behavior and comment, NaTashia nodded and said, "Okay."

Arriving at the black doormat in front of the sliding doors, I shuffled my feet before entering Glorianna's home. The last thing I wanted to do was have a word battle with the hellish bat set in her manipulative ways.

"Who's that man out there talking to my daughter, Fabian?" Glorianna snickered while a few people looked at me.

"Now, Glorianna, I'm sure you know who the man is. Hell, he came through your house," I replied in an annoyed tone.

The old broad mumbled, resulting in a select few people to laugh. Cutting my eyes at the woman, she avoided looking at me. Feeling her getting underneath my skin, I exited the kitchen. I was not known for respecting my elders, but that damn bitch worked my nerves when she shouldn't have. I tried my best to respect her, granted she was my elder. Yet, there were times I was tempted to let the miserable bitch have it.

"Aye, bruh, you good?" Cleophus asked as he scooped a spoonful of potato salad onto a white plastic fork.

Tilting my head to the side, I replied, "What do you think, nigga? Your sister knows how to work my damn nerves."

"Yes, her old ass do, which is why I'm finna blow this joint," he voiced as the back door opened.

While the lanky dude walked inside of the house, happily, he said his goodbyes. As the females sent him on his merry way, my attention was on the one it had always been on. Glaring at her kids, NaTashia had a peaceful expression upon her face. I was sure whatever the lanky nigga told her was the reason.

"Aye, we got plenty of houses to stop at. So, we out this joint," Cleophus voiced, chunking the deuces.

When we were younger, I hated it when he announced we were leaving. Now, I didn't see a damn thing wrong with it. I had the oddest feeling; I felt that today was the last day I would see NaTashia in the city. Hell, in Alabama, period. It wasn't a secret her mother didn't want her daughter and grandchildren living with her. If I was in her shoes, I would disappear as well.

"See you around, NaTashia," I softly said as I eyed her while she gazed at her children.

Placing her eyes on me, she replied, "Likewise. Thanks for giving me your listening ear."

Feeling my heart ripping in half again, I smiled politely and responded, "Any time."

Chapter Three

NaTashia

The Next Day

All night, I tossed and turned. I couldn't sleep worth a damn. I kept rehashing a particular part of my conversation with Fabian. The part about 'he could've given me the world and his last name'. As I lay in the twin bed, pondering those words, I wanted to call Fabian; however, I was sure he didn't want to talk to me. I was extremely rude to him. He didn't deserve the way I acted or spoke to him.

After I finished thinking about Fabian's words, I focused on the conversation I had with Ethan Morrelson. Ethan was Joseph's college buddy and second lawyer. I had the pleasure of being around him and his lovely wife a few times at their home during the holidays. Our children were good friends. Honestly, I was stunned to see him saunter through my mother's back door. Initially, I thought his conversation was going to pertain to what Liddia had spoken already, but it was the opposite.

"I'm sorry to disturb you as you are spending time with your family. I'm sorry for your loss, NaTashia. Hearing Joseph passed brought me to my knees. I don't know how to process it. I guess I will have to deal with it after I'm officially off a business call," he spoke as the wind blew.

"What official business, Ethan? How did you know where to find me?" I questioned as I kept looking towards the sliding door; I was sure Fabian was close by. He wasn't, which made me a little sad.

"Joseph loved you more than you will ever know. In the beginning stages of your and Joseph's relationship, he had me complete a background check on you. He felt as if you didn't give him anything to go off of. Basically, he wanted to know more about you. So, I had this address on file for you. As far as my official business, it's to deliver these documents to you," he spoke with a small smile on his light-skinned, long oval-shaped face.

"What is this?" I asked, retrieving a thick and large brown envelope.

As I took a seat and opened the envelope, Ethan took his time explaining everything I saw. Overwhelmed, tears slipped down my face. My heart was overjoyed. My children and I would be okay.

As I held tightly to Joseph's stationery paper, Ethan said, "That's a letter. I haven't read it, but Joseph told me when he handed me these documents years ago, there's important information in there you should know."

After ensuring I was okay, Ethan sat beside me as I read the letter.

My Sweet Face,

I'm sorry you are enduring this pain. I never wanted to hurt you or our children. The three of you mean the world to me. You are going through the worst times any person should be going through. You won't be hurting for long. Don't hate me for what you have learned. Many times I asked Liddia for a divorce, and she declined. I've gone so far as to send her divorce papers. She never signed them. I tried to legally separate from her, but she has people in high places that threw those papers away. She stopped me from being with you the way I should've. I will always take care of you and our children. I have set up accounts for them. Each one will have their own banking account. They can't touch it until they are twenty-two. In the meantime, I have left you a large lump sum of cash to care for them until they come of age. When I first met you, you had your eyes set on being a fashion designer. Like I told you many times before, I can get you through the door. Just use the contacts enclosed in this letter. Shine bright like a diamond, My Sweet Face. Kiss our children for me every day and night. Let them know just how much I love them. I'll always be looking down on you three.

P.S. My Sweet Face, don't let what I did stop you from loving again. You deserve the world and then some. You are such a beautiful soul. Give that love to someone deserving of it.

Yours Forever,
Joseph Minnow

I re-read the letter four times before I asked Ethan what I should do or if I should tell the children their paternal family members didn't want anything to do with them?

"Nope. Why tell them anything of that nature if they were told from babies their father didn't have any family?"

It was apparent Ethan knew everything that was told to me. Instantly, I felt like a fool. I wanted to be angry, but Ethan's choice of words ceased those feelings. I was a whirlwind of emotions, and I didn't know how to feel or react to any of the shit I had been in. I couldn't understand how I was supposed to be okay with being lied to by the man I swore would be my husband one day. The same man who had given me two beautiful children I love more than anyone in this world.

"Are you okay, NaTashia?" Ethan asked as he stood.

Nodding, I replied, "I will be. Thank you for coming."

"If you need anything, please don't hesitate to ever call me, NaTashia," Ethan soothingly voiced as we embraced in a hug.

"Okay."

Strolling through the front door, loud as ever, Cleophus knew how to cease me from thinking.

"Shit, niece, you look like shit. What's on your mind?" he asked, taking a seat next to me.

"Life," I replied as I sat Indian-style on the She-Devil's couch.

"It'll be okay. Just be 'round the one who makes you smile an' feel worthy. I know my sister can be a hard-up woman. She will never change. Just break free an' stay free this time. I've tried talkin' to her, but it goes into one ear an' out the other. You know old people don't like to listen to anyone younger," he voiced before pausing and then continuing, "I tell you what— link up wit' Fabian, an' I'll take my niece an' 'phew shoppin'. Don't worry, my guh, Santana, will be wit' me. She'll be 'the' responsible adult. You know I can act like a big kid wit' kids."

Shocked, I said, "Your girl? Since when does my uncle have a girlfriend?"

"Since I found the sexy damsel walkin' onto Alabama State University campus fo' years ago. Niece, you are going to love her. She's the best female any nigga could've asked fo'."

"Is that so?" I stated, eyeing him.

"Very much so."

With a smirk on my face, I nodded and replied, "Okay."

"Anything I need to know 'bout them, allergies per se?" he asked as I heard Momma fussing.

Hopping to my feet, I quickly said, "Nope. Please get them out of here before I snap her damn neck about my kids."

"Say no mo'."

Thirty minutes later, my children and I were out of the door. Cleophus dropped me off at Fabian's house. Thanks to Fabian, when I turned fifteen, he had given me a spare key, against his mother's knowledge. Upon opening the screen door, I prayed I didn't walk in on anything I didn't need to see. I wasn't a fan of popping up at people's houses. Yet, here I was strolling through the cozy place, which I had secretly referred to as home.

The single-family home belonged to his late parents. Fabian's father passed away in a job-related accident when he was eight years old. I never got the chance to meet the highly praised man, but they talked about him enough to the point I felt as if I knew him. Fabian had modernized the house, but it still had Mrs. Lola's touch. On the walls were pictures of Fabian's parents, along with a few photos of us when we were teenagers. As I touched the images, happy moments slammed into my head, resulting in me lightly giggling.

"The good old days," I said, walking towards the master bedroom. There was no doubt Fabian had taken one of the two most oversized rooms within the four-bedroom house. Since Fabian was an only child-back then-I didn't understand why his parents had such a large home. When I became older, I asked Mrs. Lola about the large house. She informed me that she had hoped to have more than one child, but the day never came. So, they decided it was best to keep the house because they were sure Fabian would bring them lots of grandchildren.

As I opened the bedroom door, a smile appeared on my face as the six-foot-four, dark-skinned, fit male lightly snored as he was wrapped underneath a black cover. For a while, I watched him sleep. It didn't take me long to become annoyed with his snoring.

Stepping across the door's threshold, I yelled, "Fabian Wells, get your ass up!"

"Wha ... what?" he asked in a groggy tone, rolling onto his stomach.

Loudly, I called him by his nickname I had given him. The drunken fool didn't utter a word nor move. With a smirk on my face, I sashayed towards his bed.

As I placed my hand on his covered back, I shook and yelled, "Fabo, I said hit the damn floor!"

"For fuck sakes, Nana," he spoke groggily, throwing the covers over his head.

As I opened my mouth, Fabian threw the covers off his head. His eyes were red and bulgy. He was lost; my friend didn't know if he was dreaming or not. Thus, I helped him to realize he wasn't.

After a few seconds of staring at me, Fabian flopped onto the bed, ran his hand down his face, and asked, "Did Cleophus give you the spare key to get in?"

Rapidly shaking my head, I replied, "Nope. I used the key you had given me."

Chuckling, he said, "I thought you would've gotten rid of that key by now. It's not like you ever used it."

"Why would I get rid of the very key that allowed me to escape the hell within my mom's house?"

Shrugging, he voiced, "I guess because you didn't want anything to do with your old life."

"That's not true. I just wanted to be far away from the woman who always criticized me, my looks, my presence, and what I wanted to do with my life."

"Well, you had one hell of a way of showing it, NaTashia. Often, I sent things by Cleophus to give to you, and you rejected those items. Why?"

Shrugging my shoulders, I softly voiced, "I don't know."

"Yes, you do. I've always bought you shit, and you've never given it back. Up until the day you left, I was your best friend, NaTashia. I was always, always there for you. Why should it stop because you had a life with someone else? We vowed to be best friends for life."

"I know," I stated, avoiding looking into his eyes.

"I'm going to assume he never knew you had a male best friend, huh?" I asked.

"No."

"Wow," Fabian voiced before sighing heavily and looking away.

"I didn't want him to think negatively towards a woman and man being close friends. I sure as hell didn't want him to feel as if I would step out on him. I'm sure you can understand that," I softly voiced, placing my eyes on him.

"Yeah," he replied in a dry tone.

Instantly, I saw how badly I had hurt him. I tried to find the right words to say, but nothing came out of my mouth. The feelings of shame crept through my body as I realized I was the worst type of person to him. We had vows we made to each other, and I didn't honor any of them; yet, he did. I missed many important moments in his life; I felt terrible then. Now, I felt worse.

"Fabo?" I called out, fumbling with my hands.

"Yeah?" he responded, eyes closed.

"I'm sorry I didn't come back to be here for you when Ms. Lola died. There aren't any excuses as to why I didn't come. I guess I was a selfish bitch."

"Yeah, you were."

"What can I do to make that up to you?" I lowly voiced, eyes fixated on him.

"Nothing."

"Not even me staying in the city would make that up to you..."

As he opened his eyes, a huge grin was plastered upon his handsome, dark-skinned face. Just as quickly, Fabian had smiled, it disappeared.

"Like I said, there's nothing you can do. All is forgiven, Nana."

While we glared at one another, I kicked off my shoes and snuggled under the cover with him—as I had done so many times when we were younger.

"Fabian!" I hollered before laughing.

"What, woman?" he chuckled.

"Put on your boxers, at least." I blushed at the image of seeing his *grown* naked, perfectly crafted body.

"Woman, you came into my house while I was sleeping. Do you honestly think I'm going to put on my boxers? I mean, if you want to be technical, you've seen what I have to offer. So, stop acting, woman," he stated with a raised eyebrow.

Rolling my eyes, I responded, "Whatever, dude."

A brief silence overcame us as I looked at the ceiling, and he looked at me. There was no doubt there was mad energy between us; hell, it had always been there. Yet, I refused to allow us to become anything other than what we were—friends with no benefits.

I couldn't lie; there were many times I wanted to have nasty yet passionate sex with Fabian. Like he stated, I did have the pleasure of seeing what he had to offer. It was indeed something to test out. His penis had the right length, girth, and curve, just for me.

Clearing his throat, Fabian asked, "Why did you come over, Nana?"

"Because I hadn't been here since Mrs. Lola was the owner of the house. Plus, I wanted to be near my friend," I voiced, glaring into his eyes.

"Oh," he stated as if he didn't believe me.

Profoundly sighing, I sat upright in the bed. While I positioned my legs to pose in an Indian-style position, I spoke, "Fabo, I haven't been a good friend to you. Truly, it saddens me deeply that you've always gone out of your way for me, and I haven't for you. It saddens me that the only person who hangs out with my uncle always gave me his best and I half-assed gave my all to him. You are my true friend. I never had any girlfriends worthy enough of being in my life. It was always you. For as long as I can remember, it was always you and me against the world. After I received some items from my children's father's friend and lawyer, I had some time to reflect on the letter from Joseph and what I want my life to be like. For me to do that, I need my friend along the way. The person I've known since I was seven years old. The one who pushed me off the swing, resulting in me busting my damn knee, and creating a beautiful friendship."

Laughing heartedly, Fabian replied, "I received the worst ass whooping of my life. To this day, I think there is skin missing off my cheeks."

"I think so too. Mrs. Lola didn't play the radio with you."

Placing his head in my lap, Fabian said, "She surely didn't play the radio about *you*. Up until her death, she always told me never to hurt you, and if I did, she would haunt me until the end of times."

Knowing we were heading into a touchy topic, I braced myself for the impact.

Looking at the ceiling, he said, "Momma swore up and down you were going to be my wife someday. Did you know she knew you were here during the wee hours of the morning on school nights?"

Shocked, I shook my head and said, "Now, that I didn't know. I was careful when I entered and left. How did she know?"

"We would fall asleep, and neither of us heard her come into my room," he chuckled.

"Oh, wow." I smiled as I dipped off in memory lane.

My momma was a real terror in my life. She was an old-school woman and handled me accordingly, or it could've been she disliked everything about having me without a man in her life. Either way, I received the backend of what my 'unknown' dad presented to her. Momma kept a roof over my head, clothes and shoes, and food to feed my belly. She never gave me the love I yearned for. Hell, she barely gave me love, period. To me, I was a burden, and she couldn't wait until I was out of her presence.

Upon hitting puberty, staying under my mother's roof had become unbearable; she was rude and nasty for no reason. It seemed as if I was her slave and personal doormat. I never received anything I wanted; it was always what I needed. My room wasn't a safe haven from her harsh words and stern punishment. I couldn't wait until she found sleep in her room underneath many covers; that was my only chance to sneak out of the house and find comfort and peace within the walls Mrs. Lola had created. Plenty of nights, Fabian held me as I silently cried. Many days before school, he was the one telling me everything would be okay.

"You and my godkids can move in with me if you would like. As you know, I have more than enough room. These walls are a tad bit lonely," he voiced, looking up at me.

With a raised eyebrow, I asked, "Now, how that would look, especially with kids aged eight and ten?"

"Guh, be quiet. You act like we are fucking. I have my own room, and everybody will have their own room. The kids are free to decorate their rooms in any way they like. I don't shit where I lay, meaning I don't conduct any illegal business here. I don't allow for it to be talked about within my walls. There are no bitches running in and out of my place. Hell, I go to their place. One thing Momma taught me was to never have women sauntering around my safe haven place if I don't see a future with her," he said as his phone rang.

Gazing into his medium-beaded eyes, I replied, "Hold up, your godkids?"

Laughing, he said, "You still listen slow as fuck, huh?"

Playfully slapping him across the forehead, I replied, "Shut up. You know I have a thing for barely listening."

"Some things never change, huh?"

Shaking my head, I replied, "Not at all. Now, back to this godkids thing."

"What about it, and where are they?"

"Cleophus and his lady friend took them shopping," I replied before continuing, "Who said anything about you being their godfather?"

With a raised eyebrow, he pointed at the nightstand a few inches away from the bed.

"Why are you pointing over there?"

"Look in the top dresser, and you'll see exactly what you need too."

As I oddly looked at him, Fabian continued ordering for me to open the top drawer. Upon doing so, I laughed and shook my head.

"You kept this?" I questioned, shocked.

"I did," he quickly replied before saying, "Close your eyes. When you hear the bathroom door close ... open your eyes and read. It's not appropriate for my new roommate slash best friend to see me naked."

"Boy!" I hollered as I did what he commanded.

Upon hearing the door close, I opened my eyes and placed them on the green, 5-subject notebook that held our names and other doodles. Flipping open the notebook, my eyes became teary as I read the words *Nana & Fabo's Friendship List Requirements.* There were several things on the list, yet there were only four items that caught my attention: *#6, we will be godparents to each other kids. #7, we will always be there for each other. #10, we will always be friends before anything else. #12, when one is in need, the other will always be there to help. #14, we will always have a bond like no other; no one will ever tear us apart.*

As Fabian turned on the water in the tub, I felt more disappointed in myself as I overlooked the five major things we had agreed on at the age of thirteen.

I didn't fulfill those five essential requirements, yet Fabian didn't break a single rule, I thought as I placed the book in the top drawer.

I hopped out of bed and aimed towards the master bathroom. Upon knocking several times, Fabian hollered for me to come in.

As I opened the door, my eyes fell on him, sitting on the toilet and cuffing his dick. It wasn't the first time I witnessed him taking a shit; thus, it wasn't anything for me to close the door behind me and plop on the sink, all the while looking at him.

"Fabian, I'm really sorry for not honoring anything we had written down. I'm sure you don't forgive me for leaving you high and dry when you needed me the most, but I promise you I'm here now, and I'm going to make up for it. My life isn't in Atlanta or any other city. My life is wherever my children are. I'm sure I have to learn the "grown" you as you have to know the "grown" me. I don't want to miss another minute out of your life. Okay?" I stated, voice breaking.

Nodding, he replied, "Okay."

"So, where do we start?" I questioned, covering my nose.

Busting out laughing, Fabian said, "By you spraying the air freshener until it's nothing left while you tell me about my godkids, Angel and Maxon."

Dropping my hand from my face, I smiled, "That'll be a pleasure."

Chapter Four

Fabian

Today had been a great day. I spent it with NaTashia. Everything we wanted to do, we did. It was as if we were teenagers. There wasn't an uncomfortable or lousy moment; only laughs and a great ride down memory lane. I was beyond excited to meet Angel and Maxon. While Maxon was skeptical of me, Angel was smitten with me. Two hours after having them in my presence, Maxon's mood softened, resulting in the dark-brown, curly head, sports fanatic kid talking to me as if he had known me all of his life. Being the goofy brat she knew how to be, NaTashia showed the kids old photos of us, dating back to our school holiday parties. Maxon was in shock that a boy and girl could be best friends. Angel frequently stated she couldn't wait until she had a boy for her best friend. Once the photos were put up, Maxon and Angel asked more questions concerning our friendship. NaTashia and I didn't mind answering any of them. It was refreshing to hear her profound love for me as her friend.

The second part of our day had me eager for tonight's event. Every year for as long as I could remember, the Friday after Thanksgiving, the crew and I found ourselves inside of someone's club. Tonight wasn't going to be any different except NaTashia was going to be present. After lunch, I presented her with the event, and I had a battle getting her to agree to come. With every excuse she threw at me, I slammed a solution in her face. Around five o'clock p.m., she caved in to my begging antics. Immediately, I was like a greedy kid at a buffet, smiling and overly happy.

I had the best babysitter in the world, eager to spend time with my godkids, my Auntie Marilyn. Like my mom, Auntie Marilyn loved NaTashia and always wondered why we never became a couple. Hell, even I pondered that, but I didn't say anything to NaTashia about it. It wasn't like I didn't throw hints out at her; honestly, I never stopped. In due time, NaTashia was going to see that her knight in shining armor had been in her face, all along.

"Um, so do I have to dance?" NaTashia inquired with a worried expression on her face, tugging on her suspender, plaid shorts outfit.

Pulling into the packed parking lot of the nightclub, I laughed, "What kind of question is that woman?"

"A legit one. I hadn't *really* danced in ages. I don't think I know how."

"So, you telling me you never twerked for the dude?"

"Nope."

"Not once?" I probed, parking beside Cleophus's truck.

"Not a single one."

"Did y'all slow dance?"

"Sometimes."

"Wow. I guess I will help you get back to the old you. No offense," I stated as I noticed a trail of smoke coming out of Cleophus's truck.

Giggling, she replied, "None taken."

"Now, when we get in here … off the rip, we take six shots."

"What!" she hollered, shocked.

Nodding, I replied, "Non-negotiable, Nana."

"Oh, so I'm going back to my kids wasted," she voiced with a raised eyebrow.

"They will be sleep by the time we return."

"Wait, so you saying we will be out all night?"

Laughing, I nodded and said, "Yep."

"I really should've thought this through," she smiled.

At the same time, we saw Cleophus standing in front of his car, doing the 'beat it up' dance.

"I see my uncle hasn't lost his spunk, huh?" NaTashia laughed.

"Not a fucking bit. You would think the older he got, the more grown-up he would act. Shid, not that nigga, the ladies love seeing him come in the club. That negro be dancing his ass off and dare somebody to say some to him."

As I saw the crew and their groupies filing out of their vehicles, we followed suit.

"I thought Fabian was lying when he said he got you out the house, niece!" Cleophus laughed as he hugged the one who held my heart.

"He owes me big time," NaTashia responded, looking at me.

"You know he gon' cash out, guh. You still his lil' buttacup," Cleophus stated thoughtfully.

Rolling her eyes, NaTashia replied, "Now, I don't know about that."

"Shid, you should. It ain't like he been hidin' it. Better open them big, dreamy ass eyes an' clean out those ears," Cleophus fussed while many female fans of mine spoke to me before sashaying inside of the club.

One person said 'shots' and I be damned if the cups and several rounds of shouts of "shots" sounded off. Before we entered the club, seven shots were down, and the welcoming sensation of alcohol flooded through my body. NaTashia's body became less tensed as she stood beside me. The liquor was talking to her, which brought pleasure to me. I didn't want her to feel out of place; she wasn't familiar with the clubbing scene or us. She had no idea just how powerful our crew was. She had no idea that we were certified killers, but she knew we were massive dope sellers.

Inside of the club, King South's "Yo' Body" blasted from the speakers. Instantly, Cleophus did what he knew how to do, act a fool with his girlfriend, Santana.

Loudly, my partner spat, "Guh, it's time to head in so I can see you move that body."

"Fall out!" I shouted, pointing towards the door of the club.

Just like that, we were on the move inside one of the nightclubs we had secretly invested our money in. We didn't like to be in the limelight of police officers' and bullshit. Therefore, we paid the club owner to employ top-notch security guards to ensure there weren't any bullshit going on inside or outside the club. We didn't conduct sales on the grounds. Along with many hardworking people, we needed a place to relax after a long week of hustling. Also, we helped him rebrand the business.

If the person interested in stepping foot inside the club wasn't thirty or above, they couldn't enter. The club made massive money and was always the best place to be.

"I'm nervous," NaTashia voiced as we stepped onto the concrete walkway.

"It'll go away once you become comfortable."

"Once inside, please don't tell me you are going to leave me, Fabo," she lowly asked, looking at me.

"Not for a single moment ... well, unless I have to piss." I smiled.

Shaking her head, she giggled, "Classic. So you."

Upon entry into the club, the DJ had the blues songs on wham. I jigged to them, and NaTashia seemed as if she was bored while sipping from a white, plastic cup. She had never been a fan of blues music. She was more into rap, love, and twerking music.

"Pocket Full of Money" by Alley Boy and Young Jeezy sounded from the speakers, resulting in NaTashia's smiling behind hopping away from the table, moving towards the semi-packed walkway.

"Okay, nih, woman!" I hollered as I bobbed my head and jigged towards her.

With a bottle of Hennesy in my hand and a blunt in between my thumb and forefinger, I stepped in front of NaTashia's swaying body.

We hollered, "Got a pocket full of money!"

Her beautiful eyes were low. She was tipsy as fuck. With a smile on my face, I had accomplished my first mission, bringing joy and fun into her life.

Together, we danced and rapped along to the song. As we stood face to face, I welcomed the fact NaTashia had breathed life back into me. It had been one lonely journey without her, and I wasn't planning on having any more lonely moments.

Once that song ended, NaTashia and I didn't see the table or chairs as I had thought; the DJ had the club jumping. The crew and I had a ball with the ladies. As usual, we upped money for the best twerker within our association. That damn Cleophus tried to enter, but we joked his ass out. Yet, it didn't stop him from jumping behind Santana as she threw her ass. At first, NaTashia was hell-bent on not dancing.

"All I Know" by Ms. Shyne, King South, & Dem Hard Headz played, and every female in our clique cut the fuck up, including NaTashia. Her drunk ass was the ringleader.

"My pussy is the fattest ... baby, I'm the baddest!" she excitedly yelled in my face with the sexiest look I had ever seen.

Yes, it is, and you are, I thought as I watched her perform the actions of the female rapper's words.

Glaring into my eyes, NaTashia seductively mouthed, "Ugh, I drop it fast, and I roll it slow!"

Oou, she lied about not being able to dance anymore, I thought as my dick hardened in my pants.

Seeing it was time for me to relax more with NaTashia, I stepped out of my element and rapped King South's part.

Pulling her close to me, I thrust my dick region and said, "I can make you cream. I can make you shout. Have you callin' my name."

Eyeing me, NaTashia sexily said, "Fabo. Fabo."

Placing my mouth to her ear, I said, "My girl."

Slowly, I removed my mouth from her ear to gaze into her eyes. They were brighter than the sun on a hot, sunny day. Those peepers of hers were my weakness.

NaTashia's chest rose and then fell slowly; she was breathing erratically. Nasty thoughts consumed my mind. I wanted to suck her bottom lip into my mouth before I tasted her tongue.

Her soft hands patting me on my chest brought me into reality. She was in a vulnerable place, and I wasn't going to take advantage of the situation or her. While glaring into her eyes, I nodded my head a few times before planting a kiss on her forehead. Shortly afterward, I stepped away from my best friend. She needed some time away from me. Every third song, we danced together.

Upon the closing of the club, the crew and I filed our satisfied behinds towards our vehicles. NaTashia was beyond drunk. Like many times before, I carried her lightweight behind to my whip and placed her in the passenger seat.

Afterward, Cleophus loudly stated, "One day, my niece will be yo' wife nigga, an' I'mma be one happy ass nigga. Two people I love the most will finally have a great ending. I love seein' y'all together. Make a nigga's heart all warm an' fuzzy an' shit."

"Maybe," I replied as I badly hoped so.

"Since you are the less drunken one, lead the way to an eatery, partna," Cleophus loudly spoke.

"Say no mo'," I voiced as I turned on my heels, aiming for the driver's side of my whip.

"Your drunk ass ain't driving me nowhere, Cleophus!" Santana laughed before continuing, "Hand me them keys, sir."

Doing as his woman commanded, my drunken friend talked massive shit. I couldn't help but laugh at the fool who punched me in the face the day I pushed NaTashia off the swing.

As I planted my body on the leather seats of my whip, NaTashia said, "Who would've thought little ole me would've brought upon a beautiful and trustworthy relationship between you and my uncle."

While starting the engine, I said, "Right. I pushed you off the swing because I lik—"

Instantly, I caught myself and started to fake cough.

"Stop that fake ass shit, dude," NaTashia laughed.

As I continued on with my antics, NaTashia leaned up and looked into my face as she asked,

"You pushed me off the swing because of what, Fabo?"

Ceasing my fake coughs, I lied, "Because I disliked you."

Busting out into laughter, NaTashia said, "You's a whole ass lie in these streets, Fabian. You were not going to say that. What were you going to really say, Fabo? Why did you push me off the swing? I'm sure it wasn't because you felt like doing it. Wasn't that the lie you told Mrs. Lola, my mom, and the school officials?"

"Yep."

"So, what was the truth of you pushing me off the swing?" she probed, gently tugging on my ear.

Fuck, I thought as she gave me the ultimate sign I had to tell the truth.

Sighing deeply, I glared into her face and said, "I pushed you off the swinger because I liked you."

Smiling, she asked, "Now, was that so hard to say?"

Placing the gearshift in the reverse position, I chuckled, "Sort of."

Along the way towards a twenty-four hours restaurant, several times NaTashia gently tugged on my ear and asked questions. Like before, I had to answer them honestly. The last one had me in a chokehold because I didn't want to ruin our friendship.

"I asked, … do you love me more than on a friendly note, Fabian?" she loudly spoke, flipping on the light and staring into my face.

Clearing my throat, I nodded and said, "Yes."

"Were you ever going to say anything about it? More so than the hints you were throwing out."

"I'm not sure."

"The day I told you I was moving to Atlanta, did you prepare a speech for me not to leave?"

Nodding, I responded, "Yes."

"Why didn't you tell it to me?"

"Because I didn't want you to fault me for not leaving. I didn't want you to be unhappy here."

"So, you let me go."

While briefly moving my head up and down, I replied, "Yes."

"Did you regret it?"

"Every-motherfucking-day."

Connecting our hands together, NaTashia said, "I'm here to stay now. I'm not leaving this time. I belong here, amongst you, June Bug, and Cleophus. Okay?"

With my eyes on the road, I licked my lips and said, "Okay."

I should've been elated, but I wasn't. I knew better than to believe anything she said while she was under the influence of alcohol. This wasn't her first time being drunk and saying things I should've shrugged off. My truths were just that, my truths. Back then, I had given her plenty of reasons to be my woman, and she chose to leave. If her mother said the wrong thing to her, who was to say she wouldn't up and leave again. I loved NaTashia true enough, but I had to tread lightly with her. She wasn't going to have me sitting on the edge of my bed, crying. She wasn't going to place me in a depressing state. She wasn't going to have me feeling as if I wasn't worthy enough to love and have her in my life as my partner. She wasn't going to get me like that again. I couldn't allow her to have that much power over me!

Chapter Five

NaTashia

November, Saturday 30ᵗʰ

As I awakened from a peaceful slumber, I stretched, feeling amazing and perky. The sun shined brightly through the dark-brown, custom blinds in the second biggest bedroom of Fabian's home. From the sounds of laughter and chit-chat coming from the front room, I smiled. My children were pleased with Fabian and Marilyn. I was surprised they took to Marilyn quickly. They weren't too trusting of people they didn't know. Fabian earned his badge by being the respectful, goofy, and fun guy that he was.

In the most comfortable flannel pajama set, I hopped out of bed, snatching my cell phone off the dresser. I didn't know why I checked the damn thing. It wasn't like I had any friends. Strolling towards the main bathroom, I noticed I had many messages from my uncle. Opening the text message, I saw many photos from last night and earlier this morning.

"Shit, I was drunk." I laughed, sauntering into the bathroom, saving every photo.

Plopping on the toilet, I eyed one photo in particular. A picture of Fabian holding me tightly as we slow danced. My head rested on his chest as his chin sat comfortably on the top of my head. His firm hands were placed on the small of my back. In that drunken moment, I knew I was in good hands. I knew I was safe from lies and betrayal. In his arms was home for me.

While taking care of my hygiene, I thought of the many years we shared together and apart. I had to admit the years we spent apart, I was indeed lonely and had become someone I never intended to be. I missed having fun and being spoiled the way Fabian had always done—time and attention. True enough, Joseph had given me everything I could ever dream of, but my little heart wasn't content. Indeed, Joseph brought plenty of happy moments, but they weren't anything like the ones Fabian had presented to me. There was always something missing between Joseph and me; it wasn't until being in the nightlife with Fabian that I realized what it was—chemistry.

That damn chemistry with black ass, I thought while exiting the bathroom and shoving my phone into the right pocket.

The closer I walked towards the front room, the more I saw what was going on. Marilyn was putting up the Christmas tree while Fabian and my kids were decorating the large front yard.

"About time you wake up, sleepyhead," the hippest auntie of Fabian's stated with a smile on her face, showing off one gold tooth.

Giggling, I replied, "I think I had one too many drinks. You know those fools can drink like a fish."

"Yes, they can," she quickly stated before ceasing what she was doing.

Staring at me, Marilyn said, "You know he puts the tree up every year in hopes you and the children will come home for the holidays. Every year since you've been gone, he places gifts and cards under the tree for you along with that damn notebook, which no one can touch. Ten years ago, he learned you had a child. He purchased two gifts for the child and two for you. From there, he always bought gifts for you and your baby. Then, you had a second child.

Nothing changed. He just added more gifts to the pile. Those gifts are still wrapped, Nana. Y'all will have a shit load of gifts to open. Many of them, the kids won't be able to wear or play with because they are out of their age range. Nana, you have no idea the power you hold over my nephew. He halted having children or being in a serious relationship because he felt you are his soul mate. Today is the happiest I'd ever seen him. The dark cloud has finally left him. However, I have to question … how long will it be before you place that cloud over him again? If you know how he feels about you and you haven't responded, why keep him feeling like he'll have a chance with you. Just be frank with him, Nana, that's the least you can do. He deserves to have a family of his own. He's far from an unattractive male, as you already know. Just set my nephew free if you can't love him the way he loves you. I'm not saying don't be his best friend, but let him know where you really stand with him. That's all I'm saying."

I completely understood what Marilyn was saying; however, I didn't know how to address Fabian. I wasn't oblivious to his feelings for me before I tugged on his ear, demanding truthful answers. I'd been known Fabian cared for me more than he let on. His actions had shown me time and time again. Like he said, he didn't allow any woman in his home; he preferred to be at theirs. Yet, it wasn't anything for me to come over without having to call. I could pop-up whenever I wanted. Even though I saw those signs and heard his hints, I still pussyfooted with becoming his partner. I didn't want us to fall out if the relationship didn't work. I didn't want to lose my best friend over an action we shouldn't have jumped in.

As I watched Marilyn put up the tree, I became nervous as my mind was in a whirlwind.

"You are fidgeting. What's on your mind, NaTashia?" she spoke, not looking at me.

"I've been in a relationship for ten years with a man who never made me feel like Fabian does slash did. However, I don't want to ruin our friendship if we don't like being in a relationship together. On top of that, I don't think it's the right time to pursue a relationship after the one I just got out of by default."

Smacking her lips, Marilyn's smart-mouthed ass asked, "And what does that have to do with you being straightforward with yourself and my nephew? The more he spends time with you and those beautiful children, the deeper he drops into the trenches."

"I think we need to go buy more lights. What do y'all think?" Fabian asked, walking towards the door.

"Yes!" my kids excitedly yelled, causing me to smile.

While Fabian walked across the door's threshold, he had the most beautiful smile on his face. "Ah, she's finally up."

"I am." I smiled.

"Did you sleep well?"

"Like a baby."

"Some of those crumb snatchers don't sleep well." Marilyn laughed, resulting in us chuckling.

"Um, do you mind if I take the kids to the store ... Angel wants more decorations. Plus, we are short on lights," Fabian asked, strolling closer to me.

Placing my hands on my hips, I cocked my head to the right and said, "Aren't you their godfather?"

Thrown off by my question, Fabian replied, "Um, yeah. Why ask me that?"

"The same reason I'm wondering why are you asking me can you take them to the store."

"Smartass," he playfully chuckled, walking away from me.

While watching him walk towards the back of the house, I had the need to tell him that we needed to talk. Yet, I couldn't find myself saying anything. Becoming an overly thinking person, I walked to the door. Upon arriving, I rested my head on the screen door, inhaling, and exhaling slowly.

They look so peaceful and happy. I've never seen Maxon with this much spunk. Angel, well, she's herself. Yet, there's a huge light surrounding her. My kids are happy. They are okay here.

"Is there anything y'all need from the store?" Fabian asked from behind me.

As Marilyn rattled off a series of things she wanted, I glared at the man who was actively listening. I never knew a single person who could remember an extensive list without writing anything down.

"What about you, Nana?" Fabian inquired.

"I don't think I'm ready for a relationship, Fabian. Yes, there is something deeply buried inside me for you, or it could be me pushing and keeping it buried deep. It's always been there, but I wasn't sure if it was what it was. I can trust you. Most importantly, I can trust myself with you. I would never string you along. Yet, I don't want to make a fool out of myself. I heard all of your hints. I chose not to respond. I guess what I'm saying is … I don't want to rush into anything. I want us to remain what we are, but … and … if we see fit to change the status, then we will," I rapidly spoke, surprising him.

Smiling, he said, "I can't buy that at the store, Nana."

"Shit, Fabian," I laughed and continued, "Can you be serious?"

"Sure," he spoke before continuing, "How about this? We just take it a day at a time. I'll let you lead, like always. If you don't take ahold of the ball, I won't force you. I want you to know I'm not going to always wait for you to hop on my line. That line is getting shorter and shorter, Nana, but no pressure though."

"Okay. I can respect that," I replied as I heard my mother's voice.

Quickly turning around, I asked, more to myself than anyone else. "What is she doing here?"

"We are soon to find out," Marilyn replied as my mother knocked three times on the screen door before opening it.

With a disapproving expression on her oval-shaped face, Momma sauntered in and poorly spoke to Fabian and Marilyn. Quickly, I looked at them, and their facial expressions weren't pleasant. Fabian was a few pennies short of blowing on my mother. Marilyn's plump lips were tighter than a baby's asshole.

"So, you decided to not come home last night, huh? You decided to have your kids around the next willing man to have you in his presence, huh? When are you ever going to learn to stand on your own feet? You bounce from man to man. Haven't you learned anything from the last one that upped and died with a whole wife and family? Girl, you need to wake the fuck up and become a woman who stands on her feet. I didn't raise you to be dependant on a man for anything. You are really starting to disappoint me now more than you did when you were younger. Now, get you and your kids' things and get in my car," she sternly spoke.

Fed up, I cleared my throat and asked, "How dare you come into Fabian's home and try to embarrass me as if I'm a little child, receiving any type of money from you? How dare you speak on anything you have no idea about? What makes you think I would gather *my kids* and bring them back to the very hell I escaped? You have to be out of your rabbit ass mind to think I would ever succumb them to the tortures I had to endure. We are fine right here, where we belong. As far as me bouncing from man to man, when in the hell have you ever seen me with a man? You never saw me with their father. As far as standing on my feet, you never worried about it before . . .so tell me, why are you pressed now? I'm good at disappointing, you remember. Why should my actions from last night bring you any surprise? Now, you can politely walk out of that door and not say another word to me if it's negative. By the way, you didn't raise me. Mrs. Lola did. All you did was criticize and belittle me."

As she stepped closer to me, huffing, my mother sternly spoke through clenched teeth, "I want all of y'all's shit out of my house within the next thirty minutes. Let's see if the playboy, Fabian, going to house you and your bastard children."

Before I knew it, I slapped the shit out of my mouth, twice. She didn't see it coming, and neither did Marilyn or Fabian.

"Woman, make that your last motherfucking time calling my kids out of their name. Try that shit again, and you will surely meet your fucking maker, and upon my death, I will proudly prance into the pits of hell for what I have done to you. Get the fuck out of my house!"

Realizing what I said, I didn't have time to recant.

After the treacherous woman strolled out, holding her face, Fabian said, "Well, looks like you took the ball and shot that motherfucka, Nana."

Laughing, Marilyn said, "She shot that shot, nephew. She blew the nets off that motherfucka."

Turning to face him, I glared into his face and said, "Um. I didn't mean to say that."

Stepping into my face, Fabian planted his nose on top of mine and replied, "I call bullshit. It rolled off your tongue too easily."

Rolling my eyes, I said, "Whatever, Fabian. Shouldn't y'all be getting ready to go to the store?"

"Yep. The keys to Bessie are in the counter drawer beside the 'fridge," he spoke with a smile on his face.

Awkwardly, I stated, "I hope you are not thinking I'm going to drive that chick magnet without you being in the car, Fabo. I don't feel like being harassed about you now. Today is not the day. I'll pop a bitch in her mouth."

"And I'll have the bail money." He laughed, causing Marilyn and I to chuckle.

Three minutes later, I watched my children and Fabian climb into his SUV. I was beyond surprised to see Maxon and Angel not fighting over who would sit in the front seat. Once he pulled off, I sighed heavily and shrugged my shoulders.

"See, telling him the truth didn't hurt at all," Marilyn voiced, briefly glancing at me.

"No, it didn't," I stated with a small smile on my face.

"Go ahead and get out of here. I'm sure you will have another battle with your mother. Upon your return, you must be composed," Marilyn softly said, giving me her undivided attention.

Nodding, I replied, "Yeah, you are right."

As soon as I walked off, I shouted, "Shit!"

In a worried tone, Marilyn asked, "What's wrong?"

"I don't have any clothes. All I have are the clothes I went out in."

Laughing, Marilyn replied, "Girl, if you don't get your ass in that man's room and find you a pair of gym shorts and a shirt ... I know something."

"Fabo's gym shorts are too big," I voiced loudly from the hallway.

"You better make that shit work!" she laughed.

Stepping into his room, I shook my head and walked towards the dresser that held his lounging wear. Upon opening the drawer, I smiled. He hadn't changed a bit, always proper and organized. His gym shorts were folded and placed underneath his differently hued t-shirts and muscle shirts. On top of a black muscle shirt was a piece of paper. Curious, I picked up the note and read it.

Nana, go to the bottom drawer. I'm sure you can find something in there to wear.

"When did he write this letter?" I asked with a small on my face as a bubble surged through my stomach.

While balling up the paper and throwing it in the small trash bin beside the small dresser, I opened the bottom drawer. To my surprise, I saw a few pairs of jeans and shirts, all with tags on them. While pulling out an outfit, I wondered were the clothes the Christmas gifts Marilyn had spoken off.

And this is why you are my best friend and always will be, I thought as I closed the drawer.

Quickly, I dressed and prepared myself for my mother's wrath. This time I would be ready for the war she brought my way. This time I would be prepared to finally let my mother and her hurt go. She had to get out of my life for good; she was pure evil and then some. Honestly, I thought her ways would've changed with me being out of her house for so many years. I thought she would've been a better person since she was in her fifties. Learning why she hated me so much was going to be the last thing we talked about before I left her house. I didn't want to assume anything anymore; I needed answers.

Zipping out of the room, I realized I didn't have on any shoes or socks. Rapidly, I ran back into Fabian's room and retrieved a pair of black ankle socks. Since I didn't have any shoes at Fabian's house, I dashed out of the room.

"Marilyn, I'll be back soon as I can. Is there anything you need while I'm out?" I loudly asked as I retrieved the keys from the counter drawers in the kitchen.

"To come back in the same spirit that you are in. Do not let your mother kill the loving spirit inside of you. Don't let that woman get in your head about anything," she rattled off.

"Okay," I replied as I walked towards the garage door.

Upon opening the rectangular object, I glared at the covered, tricked out 1977 Buick Regal, a.k.a Bessie. A huge smile spread across my face as many memories flood my mind. Before Fabian tricked out his father's car, it was the only vehicle we had to get around in. Every morning before school, the damn car was packed to capacity, Cleophus, June Bug, their two girlfriends, and me. Many days during the second semester of our tenth grade school year, we skipped school, aiming for Pelham or anywhere not too far but far enough from home.

"And you are still up and running, huh, Old Lady? I won't bump into anything this time, Bessie. I promise," I stated as I began to take the blue tarp off the car.

While observing the green candy apple painted vehicle with expensive large rims, I felt eager to sit in the driver's seat again. Upon plopping my behind inside of the lavishly gutted out car, I adjusted the seat and mirrors. Shortly afterward, I studied the remodeled inside. Seeing there was a button above the light, I was sure it was for the garage. Pressing the controller, the garage door slowly opened.

"Time to see what your owner has really done to you, Old Lady," I voiced as I started the engine.

Like the beast she really was, Bessie roared to life, smoothly. There wasn't a single skip in her beat. The speakers breathed, resulting in me smiling heavily. Fabian had a CD inside of the updated audio player. Our favorite song, when we were teenagers, played, and I had to start it over, all the while dropping the gearshift in the reverse position.

"Tear the club up!" I rapped along with Three Six Mafia as I slowly reversed out of the yard.

Sliding down the driveway, I saw Marilyn standing on the porch with a smile on her face. After I waved, I zoomed away from the yard, beating the block down, bobbing my head, and rapping—just like I did back in the days. As I aimed towards my mother's house, I was calm. In fact, I was relieved and content.

Fifteen minutes later, I pulled into her driveway. She was sitting on the porch, talking to her neighbors. Before exiting the car, I said a small prayer.

"Ahh, I see you in his car. Hmph, I wonder how long that shit between y'all is going to last," Momma nastily spoke as her neighbors glared at us.

"See, that's why you are lonely now. You are a spiteful woman. No wonder your siblings barely deal with you, just a nasty woman for no reason. You need to change your ways. Just grow up, Momma," I voiced before I stepped into her house.

Surprisingly, she didn't come behind me. As I gathered my children's items and packed them in the car, Momma and her company didn't say a word. Stepping into the room I had occupied, I was shocked to see my things amuck. My clothes were torn up. What she couldn't tear up, she bleached. I didn't have anything salvageable. I had gone through the worst with her, but she never destroyed my clothes and shoes. I didn't have the will to curse her out or cry. I simply shook my head as tears formed in my eyes. Refusing to let them drop, I looked at the sky and thought of my kids smiling while Fabian was close by them.

Slowly dropping my head, I cleared my throat and exited the room. I walked out as if nothing was wrong. Before I could place my feet on the porch, the woman had the nerves to look into my face and laugh. Tightly, I balled my fists. She wanted me to react to her actions; she needed me to respond. Thus, I decided not to. I glared into her face, wanting to spit in it. Instead, I swallowed my saliva.

"You want me to pop your ass, but I'm not going to. You want me to curse you out like the dog that you really are, but I'm not going to. You hate me, and I don't understand why. I never did anything to you. I stayed out of your hair, yet I still bother you. Why is that? What did the man who helped you create me do to you?" I asked, searching her eyes.

Standing, she said, "He gave me you and left me as if I didn't matter to him."

"You are pissed at me because you had to be a single mother?" I asked in a high-pitched tone.

"I'm done answering any more of your questions. Just know my hate for you run deep because of that man. I could've been anything I wanted, but I couldn't because I had to be a mother to you. I despise you because of it."

"Glorianna," her neighbors spoke disappointedly.

Honestly, I replied, "You were never a mother to me. May you have much peace and blessings in your life, Glorianna."

Turning on my heels, I strolled towards the car. Momma did what she did best throw insults at me. I didn't respond to her hurtful words. I knew who I was and what I wanted out of life.

"You will be nothing because you came from a nothing ass person!" Momma shouted as I hopped in the car.

Before dropping the gearshift into the reverse position, I turned up the radio. With the music pumping and speakers vibrating my body, I tried to tune out my mother's harsh words. However, I couldn't; those words hurt like hell. Everything she could think of to say in front of people, she did. She knew how to break my spirit. I had promised Marilyn I would come back the same way I left, but I didn't think that was possible.

Chapter Six

Fabian

I had a pocket full of money, and I was spending it left and right; I didn't mind. My ultimate dream had come true. NaTashia was back with my godkids, and I was giving them everything they wanted and needed. I knew my purpose in their lives, and I was going to fulfill it. They would never have to want for anything because I was going to get it.

While the kids strolled through the supermarket, I sent coded messages to Fabian. Upon shopping with the kids, I had the displeasure of hearing some shit in the stores that set my pressure high. I had always been the composed type, so I kept my cool as I cruised down the toy aisle, listening to the gossiping niggas, Leon and Kendrick. The more they talked, the more I wanted to bust them in their shits. One of the jokers, Leon, who sold dope for us, became too loosey-goosey with his lips; thus, I told the kids I would be right back.

Standing tall and firm, I strolled towards the yapping niggas. Once they saw me, their eyes grew big. Instantly, I placed my forefinger to my lips and sternly looked at them. Upon standing in front of them, I jacked up the one who had the most to say.

Through clenched teeth, I spoke, "I don't like niggas that talk too fucking much. There shouldn't be a soul that knows anything about what you do illegally. Move in silence, or I will fucking silence you for life. This is my first and final threat to both of you."

Releasing the stupid fool, I glared at them before I returned to Maxon and Angel. Before I exited the aisle, my angry demeanor had vanished.

Breaking me out of my thought process, Angel spoke in her natural sweetest voice, "Fabian, I think we have more than enough stuff. Don't you think?"

Chuckling, I nodded and replied, "Yes. What do you think, Maxon?"

"I been ready to go," he replied, shaking his head.

"Why didn't you say anything?"

"Because Princess Diva was having a ball, looking at dresses and girly stuff. Plus, I knew if she had everything she wanted, she wouldn't drive me insane for the rest of the day."

"Oh, hush up, Platypus," Angel spoke, rolling her eyes.

They argued, just like their mother and I did when we were younger. As I enjoyed the sibling bickering and walked towards the cash register, I wished I had the opportunity to experience the life of being an older brother. To this day, I wished Momma could've had more children.

As we approached the checkout line, my cell phone rang. Pulling it off the holster, I stared at NaTashia's number. Without any hesitation, I answered.

"Hello," I breathed.

"Hey. I need a huge favor."

"What's up?" I voiced as Angel placed her items on the belt.

"I need to borrow some money for clothes and shoes."

"You don't have to borrow it. I'll up it. How much?"

"Two hundred dollars should be fine."

Guh, two hundred ain't enough for no damn clothes and shoes. I'll give you more than that, I thought as I asked, "Where are you?"

"On Atlanta Highway. Close by the mall."

"You left Glorianna's crib."

"Yep."

"Are you okay?"

"I will be. That damn woman tore up my clothes, and what she couldn't, she bleached. That's why I need the money. I have zero fucking clothes ... down to undergarments."

Shaking my head, I had the sudden urge to shoot Glorianna in the head. It's not like she would be missed.

"I tell you what ... go to the mall. I'm sure the kids won't mind stepping off in there," I told her as Maxon placed his items on the black belt.

"Okay. How are they treating you?" she giggled.

"Pretty good, actually. Why you didn't tell me they bicker worse than us?" I smiled.

"I wanted you to see for yourself. Have they argued by who was going to sit in the front seat?"

"Nope."

"Are you fucking serious?" she inquired, shocked.

"Yep." I laughed.

"I'm so jealous. They gave me pure hell about who was going to ride 'shotgun'.'

As I laughed, the cashier eyed me. I ignored her and asked NaTashia a question, "So, are y'all going to move in with me?"

"No. I'm going to look for us a house. Um, Joseph left me money to care for us."

Glad he did the right thing by them, I was still disappointed. I didn't want them away from me.

"That's what ole boy Ethan wanted, huh?"

"That and to clear the air about everything I was told the day Joseph's wife came to the house."

Silence overcame me before I said, "Reconsider moving in with me, please."

"Fabian, we need to go slow with this."

"Understood, but reconsider. Just think about it for a while before you buy a house. Can you do that for me?"

"Yes."

"A'ight," I replied before saying, "I'll see you in a few. Gotta pay for these items."

"Okie dokie. Be safe."

"Always."

"Oh, I'll be on the side of the mall by the food court. You can't miss me, granted I'm sitting inside of Bessie."

Smiling, I asked, "How she ride?"

"Smooth."

"You didn't hit shit, did you?"

Laughing, she replied, "No, I didn't hit anything this time. Get off my line, Fabo!"

As I ended the call, I couldn't wait until I placed my eyes on that fine woman sitting in my prized car. Since Momma had given me Dad's car, there hadn't been any female allowed to ride in it unless NaTashia was in the front seat. When she left, the same rules applied. Bessie was meant for NaTashia to be inside of it, driver or passenger seat.

After I purchased and helped the kids load the bags into the buggy, we dipped out of the store. Upon arriving at the car, I thought we would never stop placing bags in the back of my SUV. I was sure the mall trip was going to be just as hellish.

"Maxon, buddy, we have one more stop to make," I told him as he climbed in the back seat.

"Are you serious?" he whined.

"Yep. We have to meet your mom at the mall, which we need to go in."

"Can we at least get some food from there?" he inquired as I started the engine.

"Most definitely."

"Then, I guess it's okay."

With a smile on my face, I left the parking spot, aiming for the only mall in the city. Along the way, I felt like a schoolboy, all over again. Quickly, I began to pray NaTashia would change her mind about moving into a house of her own.

Ring. Ring. Ring.

Retrieving my phone, I glared at a familiar number. I started to reject the number, but I knew better. The broad was going to call until I answered.

"What's up?" I voiced in the phone.

"Sooo, tell me who in the fuck is sitting your car up here at this damn mall, Fabian?" Kenya Deveraux, a freaky friend, asked.

"Who are you to ask me any questions?"

"I'm the bitch that drops pussy on you at the drop of a hat nigga. That's who the fuck I am. Now, cough up the answer!" she loudly spat.

"I only answer to one person, and that's not you."

"Well, I guess I should pull up at this car and ask the bitch myself ... who the fuck she is? I bet I will get some fucking answers!"

Anger consumed me instantly. I wanted to react, but I couldn't. What I had to say wasn't meant for children's ears. Thus, I replied, "Okay."

Ending the call, I dialed NaTashia's number. On the second ring, she said, "There's a bitch looking at me crazy. Is this the reason you are calling me?"

"Yep. I'm three lights away."

"Have that bond money ready, Fabian," she voiced before the call ended.

"Shit!" I loudly voiced as I didn't have the slightest clue as to what to do with the kids. I didn't want them to see their mother out of character.

Think. Think. Think. Fuck.

As I zoomed through the remaining lights, I decided to park away from Bessie. Turning into one of the mall's numerous parking areas, I saw my vehicle; it stuck out like a sore thumb. Thankfully, there were many parking spaces away from Bessie. I parked at the other end and told the kids not to unlock or open the car doors for a soul.

"Okay," they replied as their latest toys held their attention.

Jogging towards them, the conversation was apparent. Kenya was beyond pissed by NaTashia's calm stance. I noticed NaTashia didn't have on any shoes. Immediately, I was ready to do something foul to Glorianna for the many years she mistreated the most beautiful person, inside and out.

"Bitch, I'll pop yo' ass in the face 'bout that nigga. Yeah, I'm fuckin' him an' I have been fo' years, hoe!" Kenya yelled as she acted like she wanted to hit NaTashia.

Before I could open my mouth to tell Kenya to back off, NaTashia popped the bitch in her face, twice. Shortly afterward, NaTashia grabbed Kenya's head, pulled it down, and began giving Kenya's face a kiss with her knee.

"I've had enough of y'all hoes, always wanting to fight another female over a nigga. I don't give a fuck if you are fucking him. That's your business, bitch! What you ain't finna do is come for me because he doesn't treat you like he treats me! I am a mother of two. I don't do this ghetto ass shit, defending myself over a man I'm not even sleeping with!"

"Gotdamn, niece, wearin' that hoe out!" Cleophus shouted from a distance as I was in proximity of the women.

"Wear her ass out, niece! Wear that baldhead bitch out, niece!"

"Nigga, shut the fuck up! Get over here and help me break this shit up!" I loudly stated to my partner.

Running towards us, Cleophus said, "Hell nawl. Niece needs to get that frustration off her. Let her beat the bitch to sleep. I ain't seen her turnt like this since the tenth grade."

Shaking my head at the fool, I waited to break up the fight until there was enough space between them. There was no need in me calling NaTashia's name. She was completely gone. All she would hear was her own voice.

"I just know y'all ain't finna stand up here an' watch her damn near kill this girl!" Santana voiced as she ran up on NaTashia, trying to pull her away. That was a bad decision; NaTashia was beyond aware of her surroundings, even when her back was turned.

Within a flash, NaTashia turned around, cold-cocked Santana, all the while saying, "Bitch, don't run up on me!"

"Ah shit, niece, you don' knocked my bitch out," Cleophus voiced in a high-pitched tone, causing me to laugh.

Standing over Kenya, NaTashia spat on her before saying, "Lil' girl, you gotta do better.

Don't come for me anymore. Next time, I won't be so lenient with you."

Pointing at me, NaTashia angrily asked, "Where are my kids, Fabian?"

"In the car."

"Can we please go in this damn mall so I can get some shoes?" she asked hastily.

"Yes. I'mma go get the kids."

"Yeah, yo' black ass go do that shit, nigga."

With a raised eyebrow, I glared at her.

"You got something you want to say, Fabian Wells?" she asked with much attitude.

Hands up, I said, "Not at all."

As I walked off with a smile on my face, NaTashia said, "I always find myself beating a bitch because of you, Fabian! I'm too old for this shit! I might as well be fucking you … how these thirst traps be acting!"

I prefer we make love then fuck, NaTashia, I thought as I jogged to the car.

When I arrived in the car, I dropped the gearshift in drive and drove the opposite way of the commotion. There was a parking spot a few cars behind Bessie.

Upon parking, the kids asked, "Where is my Momma?"

Pointing towards a department store, I said, "She's standing over there."

As we exited the car, I noticed NaTashia was trying to act normal. Digging in my pockets, I gave Maxon a wad of cash.

"Give this to your mother. Now, go ahead and run across the street," I said as Cleophus called my name.

Once I saw them safe in their mother's arms, I walked toward Cleophus and a wobbly Santana.

In proximity, I asked, "Is Santana good?"

"Yeah, she gonna be alright, but that bitch on the ground needs some help," he said, holding onto his girl.

While I picked the ditzy bitch off the ground, she was moaning and groaning. I knew she was hurting like hell. That's what she got for messing with someone who was minding their business.

From a distance, we heard, "What the fuck happened to my sister?"

"There them worrisome ass hoes go," Cleophus sighed.

Kenya's sisters repeated themselves until they approached us.

"Your sister got her ass beat," I stated, looking at them.

"By the bitch who was sitting in your car, Fabian?" Nikki, the baby sister, inquired.

"Nawl, by the woman who was sitting in my car. Call her out of her name again, and I will be your fucking problem. If your sister decides to fuck with her again, that wouldn't be wise. So, I would advise y'all to get your sister and tell her to chill out," I sternly voiced before demanding them to open the back door of Kenya's car.

"Shid, you better than me, homie; I would've left the bitch on the ground and let their dusty asses put her in the car," Cleophus said nonchalantly.

"You's a nothing ass nigga, that's why," Nikki stated nastily.

"Sure is ... just like that nothing ass, musty pussy you got," he replied as I placed Kenya in the backseat.

Before I knew it, I busted out in laughter and shook my head. The other sister knew not to say anything to Cleophus; he had already shamed her in front of a crowd before. Just like her older sister, Nikki tucked her tail and walked towards the passenger door.

Keeping my eyes on the broads until they left, I asked my partner, "I'mma see you to your whip.

You need to take Santana to the hospital. Nana laid her ass out good."

"Yes, she did," he quickly voiced before asking, "Aye, you saw Nana didn't have on any shoes, right?"

"Yep," I stated before continuing, "Bruh, you need to check your sister. She did some foul shit towards NaTashia and the kids. The only reason I haven't stepped down on Glorianna about NaTashia because she's old, and she's your sister."

"What has she done now?" Cleophus sighed, glaring into my face.

As Santana moaned and groaned, all the while slowly moving her head, I informed him of his sister's antics at my house and what NaTashia told me she did to her clothes and shoes.

Shaking his head, Cleophus said, "Man, OG Buckingham did a number on my sister. He finna fix this shit, today, or I'mma blow his fuckin' head off."

Stunned, I said, "Come again?"

"You's a smart nigga. You know exactly what I said an' what it means."

"OG Buckingham is NaTashia's daddy?" I questioned, eyes wide, praying he would say no.

"Yep."

Fuck, I thought as I asked, "How long have you known?"

"I've always known. Who you think put me into this game, and why?"

"Nigga, you need to talk and fast," I told him as Santana slowly came back to life.

"He was givin' Glorianna money faithfully every week fo' NaTashia, but sis wasn't spendin' that money on her. OG Buckingham grew tired of the nonsense, along wit' beatin' on my sister because of her ways towards his third daughter. As you know, OG Buckingham is married an' have been to the same woman fo' years. OG Buckingham knew if anyone learned of NaTashia, all hell would break loose. Of course, you know his wife, Rebecca, is just as powerful as he is. So, OG Buckingham placed me in the dope game fo' obvious reasons; I knew how to hustle quietly an' to care an' protect NaTashia. Because of NaTashia, that's why we are fuckin' unstoppable to a certain point."

With a wicked smile on my face, I replied, "No partner, we are not 'unstoppable to a certain point' … we are unstoppable period."

"No, we are not. OG Buckingham's wife is unstoppable. You ain't hearin' me, man."

Firing up a cigarette, I leaned on my car and said, "Remember I told you if anything happened illegally, we would be able to get out because I possessed a Royal Flush hand?"

Oddly, he said, "Yeah."

"OG Buckingham is married to my Royal Flush hand."

"Bitch, what?" he hollered, shocked.

"Auntie Rebecca and Momma had been estranged for years because Auntie wanted to be a gangster bitch. Momma didn't want me involved with her like that, so she disowned my auntie altogether. Upon Momma's death, Marilyn took me to Auntie Rebecca and OG Buckingham's house. That day was the day I learned everything and more. That day was the day we became so powerful you didn't even know it, and I wasn't going to say anything unless I needed to." I smiled.

"Well, I be damn."

Nodding, I replied, "Right. Now, you need to get Santana home. Later this afternoon or this evening, I'm going to come over. I want to discuss in person how we need to deal with Leon and Kendrick."

"Bet," he replied as he secured Santana around his waist.

Before walking away, Cleophus said, "Nigga, I ought to bop yo' ass in the mouth fo' keepin' secrets an' shit. Are you hidin' anythin' else?"

Chuckling, I said, "Not business related nope, but personally, I'm hiding how bad I want to make love to your niece."

Shaking his head and laughing, Cleophus spat, "Shid, nigga, you better tell her ass what you want to do to her. You be pussyfootin' when it comes down to her. Drop down on her like you do them hoes. I'on know why you be actin' like you scared to speak yo' peace wit' Nana. Stop being a pussy an' tell her what you want nigga. Now, I'm gon' home to play 'Nurse Slang the Dick' 'til my guh becomes all the way conscious."

Busting out laughing, I choked on the cigarette smoke. The black bastard of a friend didn't check to ensure I was okay. Once I got my lungs right, I called NaTashia's phone.

"Hello?"

"Where are you?"

"Coming out of the mall."

Shocked, I responded, "That fast?"

"Yep. No need to be in here all day. I don't feel like doing a lot of shopping, anyway. I'm simply not in the mood."

"A'ight."

"By the way, I thought about moving in with you."

Smiling, I said, "And?"

"It's a firm no for me. Non-negotiable," she voiced, ending the call quickly.

"Fuck."

Chapter Seven

NaTashia

Saturday, December 7th

Inside of the warm and cozy home of Fabian's, Christmas music, smiling and happy children, intoxicated and dancing adults, and the aroma of tasty food was bestowed upon us. It had been years since I had felt like a little kid during this holiday season. Classmates I hadn't seen since graduation night were present with their children. Several tables were set up throughout the living room, back and front yards. Every type of game one could think of had adults laughing and talking shit. There was no bullshit or arguing of any kind—just love and happiness spreading from one person to another. To be around a group of dope selling individuals, I didn't hear any talks of illegal actions; it was all about family and friends.

As usual, my uncle was always acting a fool. He was one big ass adult-kid. If he wasn't running behind the children, he was dancing with Santana. June Bug was talking plenty of shit to some of the old heads. One of his favorite Christmas songs by The Emotions, "What Do The Lonely Do?", played. That fool hopped on the karaoke machine and sang the song to his best ability. I had to be his hype girl with my drunken behind.

Thirty minutes later, one sip of the wrong drink had me spiraling in pity. Since I had told my children of their father's passing, I had been all smiles and laughs with a super positive attitude. I didn't like that I was having fun; in my mind, I should've been upset he wasn't breathing and able to see his children grow into adult beings. I had been so consumed with my kids and my childhood crew that I simply didn't have time to mourn Joseph or overly think about it. Santana noticed I was off in a corner to myself and made me talk. Her sensible conversation had brought me out of the funk, and I didn't feel guilty anymore for enjoying life and those around me.

"Enough of this Christmas music, I wanna see som' ass shakin'!" Cleophus hollered in the microphone.

As I slapped my forehead and laughed, Fabian yelled, "I second that one, homie, but we got kids running around here."

"Man, them churren ain't stun' us. Their asses back there in the room we turned into a playroom. So, what you say homie … ass shakin' music or nah?" Cleophus probed.

Marilyn drunken tail shouted, "We finna shake some ass tonight, Cleophus! I'm with it!"

Just like that, the twerking music began. I had never laughed so hard in my life. It wasn't females my age cutting up; it was the ladies in their late forties and fifties. They were stiff than a cardboard box, but they threw their behinds the best they could. I loved seeing my older women having fun and comfortable with their bodies.

Next to cut the rug was the males. Cleophus and June Bug were the ringleaders. During our younger days, the ringleaders were involved in many fights because boys always called them faggots. To further prove they weren't, those idiots didn't mind sleeping with those boys' girlfriends and would brag about said female moaning.

"Throw that thang, baby!" Santana happily yelled, cheering her nigga on.

Once again, I laughed at my uncle's antics. He was the life of any party. He knew how to have fun, and if someone wasn't on his level, he would place them there.

"Shot time!" someone yelled from the kitchen.

"Fuck that drive the boat time!" Cleophus hollered in the microphone.

That was my cue to get my ass up and head towards the drinkers. The 1990's music dancing music was pumping loudly and had me feeling myself more than I should. The house went crazy when Luke's "It's Your Birthday" played. There were a few people strolling about who were celebrating their birthday.

"Ooouu shit! Goat mouth ass nigga! Turn that Hen' bottle loose, Fabo!" Cleophus laughed into the microphone, causing everyone to laugh.

Oh, Jesus, I thought as I squeezed between many people to arrive in Fabian's presence.

"Your turn, Nana," he sexily said, eyeing me.

People around us started chanting my name. Shaking my head, I said, "You will be cleaning up puke."

"It ain't like I haven't cleaned up your puke before. Now, shut up and drive this motherfucking boat, guh," he laughed, standing too close to me.

Rolling my eyes, I lifted up my head, opened my mouth, and stuck out my tongue.

"Shit, Nana, you got a licker on you!" June Bug hollered, causing everyone, including myself, to laugh.

"She fuck 'round an' put that motherfucka on Fabo, he gon' lose his shits fo' real!" Cleophus joked.

"Y'all wild," Fabian blushed, trying to avoid looking at me.

I couldn't say anything; I was beyond stunned at the things that left the ringleaders' mouths.

"You ready to drive the boat?" Fabian asked as "Freak It" by Lathun played.

"Yep," I responded, moving along to the beat of the song and lifting up my head.

"I know you don't like brown liquor, so I got some white for you," he spoke with a smile on his face.

"Okay."

A splash of liquor hit my tongue. I wanted to be a big girl, so I counted to fifteen before I closed my mouth. When I swallowed, it seemed as if my chest was about to run away from me.

The liquor was so damn potent I could barely breathe.

When I was able to take a breath and stop clutching my chest, Fabian nodded his head and asked, "How that moonshine taste?"

"Oh my fucking God, Fabo, you gave me moonshine? Fucking jet fuel?" I shouted, eyes wide as ever.

"Yep." He smiled while nodding.

"You are trying to start some shit, aren't you?" I asked, playfully hitting him.

Grabbing me by the waist, he placed his mouth to my ear and said, "Yeah. I won't take advantage, though. I'll be really good to her. I'll take my time, Nana. I promise."

I wasn't sure if it was the jet fuel cruising through my body or the sensual way he held and talked to me that had me purring like a kitten. Either way, I knew I had to tread lightly. I didn't want us to cross a line I wasn't ready for. Clearing my throat, I glared into his eyes. In them, I saw how happy he was. They shined bright as if they were diamonds. My best friend was happy as he should've been.

Placing my hand on the nape of his neck, I pushed on it lightly. Dropping his head downwards, I whispered in his ear, "We take it slow. Sex not necessary right now. That's what we agreed on, right?"

"Right," he voiced before lifting up his head and putting space between us.

Cleophus called Fabian towards him. As he walked off, Santana stood beside me. While we chatted, a group of females strolled into the kitchen, bouncing ass and titties. Two of them had their eyes on Fabian. They spoke with him a while before dancing on him. His ass didn't push them off; he watched them. I was fucking furious; yet, I kept my composure. I couldn't be mad or jealous. At the end of the day, I had his heart; they didn't.

"Let's get something to drink," I told Santana.

"I'm with it, but I prefer shots." She smiled.

"Then, shots it is."

After seven rounds of shots, Santana and I were in the second bedroom I was occupying, changing out of the long sleeve shirts and pants. We were drunk out of this world and hot. We needed summer clothes on our bodies, and that's precisely what we put on.

Strolling through the hallway, I felt as if I was a teenager again. I loved that feeling, being free, and having fun amongst people who loved me. Before joining the grown folks, Santana and I checked on the kids. The girls were amongst themselves as the boys played the different console video games, which Fabian, June Bug, and Cleophus purchased. After seeing the kids were okay, we danced our way towards the kitchen.

I caught the wrong sight of Fabian's hands wrapped around one of the females eyeing him; I lost my shits. If anyone was going to grind on his dick, it was going to be me. If his hands were going to be around anyone's waist, it was going to be mine!

I got something for his black ass, I thought with a smirk on my face.

Quickly, I grabbed the bottle that held the moonshine and unopened it. Lifting up my head, I tilted the bottle and counted to fifteen.

As Kilo's "Show Me Love" played, June Bug hopped on the microphone and shouted, "Now, gotdamn it, Nana. So, we doing it like that?"

Giving him the thumbs up, I swallowed the hard liquor before placing it on the table. Walking off, Santana was behind me, drinking and bobbing along to the music.

The beat to Splack Pack "Scrub the Ground" sounded off. I made it my business to pull 'Ms. Big Titties and Ass bitch' off Fabian. I had to show her how to really throw that ass on his big dick behind. Tongue sitting in the corner of my mouth, I placed my feet on the kitchen counter and rolled my ass, just like I knew Fabian liked.

"Oh shit, that old Nana is back!" June Bug hollered in the microphone.

All of my cut-up songs from back in the day played, and I gave those whores something to look at and think about. Fabian Edwin Wells was fucking off-limits. If bitches didn't know it before, they surely knew it by my dancing antics.

"I wanna fuck all y'all!" the house sang along with Alius Mafia.

Grabbing me by my throat and pulling me backward, Fabian asked, "What you got going on?"

Removing his hand from my neck, I turned to face him. "Don't get fucked up in your own house, Fabo."

Chuckling, he asked, "What you talking about, Nana?"

"Them bitches and your hands. Don't play with me. I'll knock your black ass out," I voiced, pointing my forefinger in his face.

Laughing heartedly, he replied, "So, that little stunt worked, huh?"

"Stunt?" I hollered.

Picking me up, he placed a kiss on my neck and said, "Yeah, stunt. Cleophus thought it was a good idea to ruffle your feathers a bit. I agreed. You on me, ain't it?"

Shaking my head as I rolled my eyes, I replied, "Cleophus going to get you fucked up on this very lovely night."

"I highly doubt that."

"Whatever," I replied as the music selection did a complete change.

Tank's "You Mean That Much" played, resulting in Fabian stepping away from the counter, slow dancing with me tightly holding on.

"That's what the fuck I'm talking about. Give my nephew that love he needs from you, Nana!" Marilyn shouted in the microphone.

Gotdamn they passing that motherfucker around like a hot potato, I thought as Fabian and I glared into each other's eyes.

"Outside of you being drunk, how do you feel? The situation that led you back to Alabama, being estranged from your mother, and not being with your kids' father," Fabian gently inquired.

"Thanks to Santana, putting a few things in perspective, I'm okay. I'm just taking things a day at a time. I'm starting to believe everything happens for a reason. So, I won't dwell on the past. My kids and I aren't hurting for anything. We aren't homeless. Truthfully, we are blessed and amongst the living; the living that adores us to the moon and back. I couldn't ask for more," I honestly replied.

Nodding, he asked, "You still thinking about moving into your own spot?"

"Honestly," I paused and continued, "I haven't put much thought into it. I've been looking but not actively looking."

"You are still two-sided about it, huh?"

"Yes."

"Why?"

"I guess because my mother's words did have an impact on me. I want to stand on my own for a while, just to prove her wrong."

"Why prove a miserable soul wrong when you know you can stand on your own? Earlier this week, you deposited a large cashier check in the bank. Why bother with what someone thinks, Nana?"

Shrugging, I said, "I don't know."

"Stop doing shit just to prove something to people. In that case, you are only living your life for others. Live for yourself, Nana. If you can't do anything else, at least do that for me."

"Okay."

Sternly, he voiced, "I'm serious. Stop doing that."

"I said, okay."

Cleophus summoned Fabian to him. Thus, I hopped off him and found my way towards Santana, who was playing cards with a group of old men. While I watched them play cards, my intoxicated mind zipped into a place it didn't have any business being. I tried everything in my power to keep myself from thinking about sex. I witnessed Fabian chatting with the fellas; he licked his lips, and my soul was set on fire. Every nasty thought crossed my mind, tenfold.

We are not going there yet!

"Girl, are you okay?" Santana laughed.

Looking at her, I shook my head and said, "Hell no."

"What's wrong?"

"You really don't want to know," I voiced as I eyed the bottle of moonshine.

"In that case, I know. Just go for it. It's not like y'all are strangers, NaTashia. The chemistry is there ... like super hard. Look how you acted when you saw those broads on him. You want him. Why take shit slow?"

"The only reason I'm here is because my children's father died, and all types of shit came behind that. If he didn't die, I wouldn't be here."

"Do you mean here as in Alabama or here as in Fabian's house?"

"Both."

"I'm going to call bullshit real quick, honey, especially on being at Fabian's house. If you didn't want to be here, you would've taken up your uncle's offer when you first got here. When your mother came over and showed her ass, you still could've gone to Cleophus' house. You chose not to. So, yeah, your kid's father passed away, and all that other shit happened, but you chose to be at Fabian's house for a reason. Now, you sit your pretty chocolate ass right there in that damn seat and think long and hard ... why? Shit isn't as complex as you are making it out to be. Either he's the one, or he's not; I say he is, and so does everyone in here. Y'all are really starting to make my ass itch with all this pussyfooting. Fuck, make love, and be in love, girl! Life is too short to be playing around with the matters of the heart. Now, think. Don't say another word unless someone comes and talks to you."

Twenty-five minutes later, I exited the full kitchen with a clear mind. After checking on the kids, I made my way towards the master bathroom. Deeply inhaling, I couldn't wait until I took a cold shower;

I was hot, sweaty, horny, and drunk, hot, and sweaty.

As I peeled off my clothes, turned on the water knobs, and stepped into the sparkling white tub, I was proud of the decision I made upon Santana telling me to think. Years of memories and feelings had me believing the best thing for me to do was not to think heavily about Fabian and me. Simply, I would do whatever the fuck I wanted to do, whenever I wanted to do it.

Closing my eyes while cleaning my body, I said, "I am grown. I take care of myself and children. I am allowed to make mistakes. I am must have a great life and wonderful adventures. I fucking deserve it."

As Jeezy's "Motivation 101" bumped through the house, I bobbed my head; honestly, it felt as if it was wobbling from side to side. While enjoying the song, I felt a gust of wind behind me. Rapidly, I turned around to see witness Fabian licking his lips and gazing at me as if I was a piece of juicy, pineapple baked ham.

I didn't say anything as he climbed into the shower with me. It wasn't like it was our first time taking a shower together, but it was our first time being open about our feelings for each other.

Bobby Brown's "Rock Witcha" sounded from the speakers as he stepped closer to me. My breathing became erratic as I placed my head on his chest. His hardened dick sat in the crook of my ass. Slowly, his left hand crept around my waist as his right hand traveled towards my right titty.

"I love you, Nana. I've always loved you. I'm tired of not being able to say it to your face. I'm tired of not having you as my woman. I need a life with you and not just as your best friend. I need you," he softly voiced in my ear as his hand slowly moved towards my hairless girl.

Before I knew it, I spread my legs.

"Let me love you without any boundaries, please," he begged as his thumb circled my clit and his middle finger entered me.

Panting, I dropped the washcloth and soap.

"Let ... me ... fucking ... love ... you ... the ... right ... way, Nana," he slowly and provocatively stated as his finger tapped against my G-Spot.

My knees buckled, but his firm hand on my waist ensured I didn't fall. Biting my bottom lip, I whimpered as if I was a hungry kitten.

"Nana?" Fabian stated as he kissed and sucked on my neck.

"Yes," I cooed, placing my leg on the soap dish.

"I love you," he said, fingering me faster.

My eyes rolled in the back of my head as I tried to tell him I loved him also.

"Fabiannn," I whined as I came on his finger, along with tears welling in my eyes.

"Yes?" he voiced, nibbling on my ear.

He continued playing in my girl before savagely turning me around and pinning me up against the wall. As we glared into each other's eyes, everything made sense.

The moment is right. It is time we take this step, I thought as I wrapped my arms around his neck and softly said, "I'm ready for you, Fabian."

"Many females are ready for me, Nana. I don't want you ready. I want you to fucking need me. I need you to love me. If you don't need or love me, I can't do this. I can't give you my all if you ain't in it," he genuinely spoke.

As I pushed him away from me, I glared into his eyes. They had shown he was afraid. Standing in the middle of the tub, I dropped to my knees as I seductively gripped his dick. My eyes never left his face as I made love to his penis with my mouth, and my hands alternated between caressing his balls and jacking his monster of a tool.

Without much thought to it, I gave my best friend something I never gave my children's father, the best oral sex I had to offer. I was never a fan of sucking dick, but I had always fantasized about sucking, followed by swallowing Fabian's nut.

"My God. You don't like to suck dick. You hate that shit, but you are sucking me up," he moaned, gripping the back of my head as his toes curled.

I enjoyed the act so much that it turned me on. Every little trick I thought I couldn't do, I did.

"Nana, I'll kill about you," Fabian stated through clenched teeth before he loudly groaned.

As I was lost in twisting my head, blowing, moaning, and humming on the dick, Fabian did a lot of talking, which I knew he would fall through on. I removed my hand off his dick, glared into his eyes, and gave him the nastiest and sexiest head he would ever receive in his life.

"Marry me, Nana! Marry me, please be my wife. Soon," he begged as tears slipped down his face.

The vein in his dick grew. He was on the brink of nutting. Rapidly, I hit that head with much passion and dedication.

"Oou, I'm finna cum, Nana," he moaned, squirming.

With a mouth full of dick, I said, "Hannit hea, Fabian. Hannit hea."

Mouth hanging open and eyes bucked, Fabian couldn't say anything as I sucked and swallowed every ounce of nut he had to give me.

Upon me standing, I licked my lips and said, "Yeah, you taste better than I thought you would."

Stunned, he said, "Come again?"

"That's a story for another day. Don't we have guests to entertain? We should get back to them." I smiled.

"Guh, fuck them, folks. Cleophus, June Bug, and Santana got them covered. Auntie Marilyn and a few of her friends will keep an eye on the kids. You and I need some alone time. Yeah, you showed me you love me, but I need to hear that shit," he voiced, pulling me closer to him.

"And *just* how are you going to get me to say it?" I sexily asked before biting my bottom lip.

"You are going to find out soon as I get you out of this tub," he stated, lifting me up.

Once in the bedroom, I looked towards the door.

"It's locked," he handsomely stated, placing me on the bed.

Spreading my legs, I nervously replied, "Okay."

"No, Nana, don't sound like that," Fabian sternly said.

"Okay," I voiced in a more chipper tone as I watched my best friend drop to his knees.

I observed him watching me as his long and wide, pink flesh slowly exited his mouth. As my fingers twitched, I held my breath. Fabian French-kissed my pussy, resulting in me screaming his name. The more he tongued my pussy down, the more those three little words were on the brink of escaping my mouth. I wanted to give him a run for his money, but I was going to fold the way his mouth was set up.

Shaking his head as if he was a pit bull and sucking on my clit, I hollered, "Fabian, I've always loved you and not just because you are my best friend. I love youuu. I need youuu and only youuu. The kids and I are not moving into our own house. We are going to stay and build with you. We deserve to be happy together."

Removing his mouth from my precious girl, he asked, "Where will you be sleeping at, Nana?"

"In here, the fuck," I shot back, causing him to laugh.

"What are we going to tell the kids?"

"We in a relationship together, the fuck you mean," I replied as his finger entered me.

"When we going to do that?" he sexily asked, picking up the speed of his finger.

"Tomorrow morning," I cooed.

"My girl." He smiled before planting his face in my wet and succulent pussy.

Chapter Eight

Fabian

The Next Day

We missed the rest of the holiday party. Neither of us seemed to mind. Cleophus didn't either, as his foolish ass interrupted us just to say he and Santana were staying over. We didn't mind at all; honestly, their presence of staying over was highly welcomed.

For the first time since we had become adults, we spooned as a couple. I had forgiven her for leaving me seventeen years ago. I had forgiven her for having children with another nigga. Finally, I had made love to the only person I ever wanted to. I didn't want to sex or fuck her; she would get that in due time. Once my sacs were emptied, I enjoyed watching NaTashia go to sleep with a massive smile on her face. Upon hearing her softly snoring, snuggled closely in my arms, I was one happy guy dosing off.

Several times throughout the wee hours of the morning, we had another steamy, excellent round of touching, kissing, licking, and making love. She was thirsty, and I was starving.

I had to say this year was the best year I had in a long time. It was all because of my Nana. She restored life into me. She brought me back from the dead; honestly, I thought the nightmare wasn't going to end.

Ring. Ring. Ring.

"Hello," NaTashia whispered into her phone.

I wasn't asleep, but I wasn't awake, either. My soul required more of her. However, I didn't want to exhaust my girl.

"No, he's asleep," she softly said before replying, "I'm thinking about it, but um, this time, I want to get nasty and loud. Can't do that . . . the kids will hear us."

And here I thought I would exhaust her, I thought with a smile on my face.

"Y'all can take them wherever y'all want to when they wake up," she happily voiced.

After a few soft laughs, NaTashia ended the call before placing her phone on the nightstand. I didn't move or open my eyes. I wanted to know was she going to make the first move. She did, and it was everything. I felt her warm body gliding across mine. I felt her gentle hands touching my body as she planted kisses from my stomach until she reached my happy guy; he was up.

Just as she was about to inhale him into her mouth, I flipped her onto the bed and said, "Don't say a fucking word. You want it nasty ... I can give you that, but you can't be loud. So, this is what I propose ... I stuff a sock in your mouth. I bind your wrists together with a belt. I give you some of what you want. When the kids leave with Cleophus and Santana, I'll give you exactly what you are seeking."

"Okay." She smiled.

I popped her thigh as I glared at her sternly. "I thought I said don't say a fucking word, Nana."

The sexiest and most exciting expression was plastered on her face as she bit her bottom lip.

"You are going to drive me more insane. You know that?" I voiced before planting a kiss on her lips.

She didn't respond, but NaTashia nodded her head.

After I retrieved a pair of socks and a belt, I began to bind her wrists to the headboard post. I was on the verge of stuffing the socks in her mouth when I found the will to ask her a question.

"Did *he* ever do things like this with you?"

"No."

"May I ask why?"

"Because I never asked."

"Why is that?"

"Because I didn't want him to. I always wanted you to do this," she replied, glaring into my eyes.

"For how long, Nana?" I inquired with a raised eyebrow.

Blushing, she voiced, "When I saw how you had Nanette Lawson in your room on Halloween night."

Stunned, I glared at my best friend while a super old image surfaced, like a tenth-grade type of old thought. Nanette Lawson was one of my experimental sexual friends. That girl and I had engaged in some enjoyable sexual activities. She turned me onto bondage and dominance. I wouldn't say I was a Dom or anything, but I liked having a woman tied up.

"Did you feel some type of way by seeing that?"

"Yep."

"Why you didn't tell me?"

"Because you were my best friend. In my mind, we were strictly friends ... no hanky panky business."

Dropping my mouth to her titty, I twirled my tongue around the hardened, Hershey kiss shaped nipple. After I sucked on it right, I slowly removed my mouth and said, "I would've given you everything you wanted, Nana. All those bitches I was fucking with, they would've been gone the second you hinted you wanted me. All you had to do was open your mouth and told me how you felt."

Silence overcame us as I had one more question left to ask. I cleared my throat several times before I asked, "Did you leave here a virgin, Nana?"

Biting her bottom lip, she nodded and said, "Yes."

"Why?"

"Because you didn't pop my cherry, Fabian. Honestly, I always thought you would've been the one to break my hymen," she spoke in the sweetest voice.

Instantly, I felt a surge of anger soar through me. I was angry at myself for not listening to Momma, Cleophus, and the rest of the fellas. I was mad at her for not stepping up when she knew I wasn't going to. I was pissed off at the nigga who took her virginity.

Resulting to silence, I indicated for NaTashia to open her mouth. Once she did so, I gently placed the sock inside of her wet mouth. Slowly rising off her, I kicked the covers to the bottom of the bed. As I eyed the beautiful creature in my bed, I lowly growled. While she cooed, I paid attention to the rise and fall of her chest.

I didn't know what I wanted to do first; therefore, I stood on my knees, thinking. NaTashia was antsy. Either she wanted to know what was on my mind or when the show was going to start.

Picking up her legs and placing the heels of her feet on my chest, I sucked on her toes, nice and slow. I catered to those average-sized feet for a while before I licked her legs until I arrived at her sweet-scented jackpot. I sniffed, inhaled, and gobbled the pussy, all the while exploring her insides.

From underneath the sock, a series of sexy, muffled noises informed me NaTashia was being pleased, the right way. Even though it had been a long time since I had put my tongue to use, outside of recent moments, I worked that skillful pink flesh as if my life depended on it. Against and inside of her pink folds, I wrote my name in cursive and print. I didn't hesitate to place today's date. If I had known the time, I would've written it.

"Ugh," sounded from her mouth as she wrapped her legs around my neck.

Taking things a step further, I ceased my actions. As I exited the bed, aiming for the bathroom, I was sure my girl wondered what I was up to. Not too quickly, I brushed my teeth and gargled with a minty mouthwash.

In the mirror, I smiled and thought, *Time to make her crazy for sure.*

Sauntering back to my room, I turned on the TV. I didn't want music playing; I didn't want the kids to think anything odd. Thus, I placed it on YouTube. With my favorite playlist selected, I put on the only thing that helped me sleep peacefully. As the thunderstorm sounds blasted from the surround sound system, I strolled towards the bed. I freed her hands from the belt before I removed the sock out of her mouth.

"You said you wanted it nasty and loud, right?" I inquired, climbing between her legs.

"Yes."

"Well, you can sort of have it," I savagely spoke as I placed her legs beside her head and blew on her hairless pussy.

"Jesus!" she loudly spat, eyes wide.

Like the nasty nigga Nanette taught me to be, I showed my best friend and future wife why she would be super crazy about me. I showed my one and only I would never disappoint her when it came down to our lovemaking. After I devoured her pretty kitty, I was ready to take her on the ride of her life, up against the wall. As she inhaled my bottom lip into her warm mouth, NaTashia whimpered and whined.

Arriving at the desired destination, a smile was on my face as I inserted my starving dick into her drenching honeypot. As I slid the head of my dick into NaTashia's pussy, that monkey of hers did numbers as she worked it so wonderfully.

"Fuck me, Fabian," she cooed as several loud knocks sounded at the door.

We ignored it.

"Fabian, have you seen my mom?" Angel asked as if she was on the verge of crying.

"Shit," NaTashia said, slapping her face.

As I removed my man from its home, I whispered, "What do I do?"

Lowly, she laughed, "Fix the bed, get in the bed, and act like you are asleep. I'll do the rest."

While I did what she said, NaTashia quickly put on a pair of my gym shorts and a large T-shirt.

As I rapidly fixed the bed, Angel knocked on the door loudly and yelled, "Fabian! Have you seen my mom?"

Muting the TV, NaTashia looked at me and sleepily said to *our* daughter, "Angel, I'm coming, honey. Hold on. Mommy had too much to drink. Please stop yelling before you wake up everyone else."

With a smile on my face as I hopped in the bed, I thought, *oh, you are an actress too, huh?*

Once I was underneath the covers and pretending to be asleep, my bedroom door opened.

"I was looking for you everywhere, Mommy," Angel softly stated, relieved.

"I'm right here, baby. Come on and let me put you back to bed," NaTashia voiced as if she had a hangover.

"I don't want to go back to my room. I want to curl up in between you and Fabian."

I'm already in love with that little girl.

"Um, I don't think that's a good idea, sweetheart," NaTashia spoke.

Whining, Angel asked, "And why not, Mommy?"

"Fabian and I had too much to drink. We might vomit all over you, baby. I don't think you want chunks of vomit on you. Do you?"

"Eww, no, I don't," Angel stated in a grossed tone.

"How about this, we all snuggle up later tonight and watch a movie in here?"

Happily, Angel said, "I like that idea."

"Okay. I see it's seven o'clock, Angel. You really need to get some more rest. You don't want bags under your eyes, right?"

"Right," she stated before asking, "Can you put me to bed, Mommy?"

"Sure. I have to use the bathroom. I will be in your room shortly. Okay?"

"Okay."

My bedroom door closed, and I didn't open my eyes. I wasn't sure if Angel was still present. In the bathroom, the water ran. A few times NaTashia spat. It didn't take me long to figure out what she had done.

"You can stop acting like you are in a casket. Angel has left the room," NaTashia laughed.

Chuckling, I opened my peepers and glared at the beauty with remnants of toothpaste in the corner of her mouth.

"Wipe your mouth, baby," I softly spoke, dick growing.

After doing so, she said, "Thanks. I'll be back once I get her comfortable in bed."

"Your breath wasn't hot, you know."

"No, it wasn't, but I didn't want to kiss my daughter on the forehead, nose, and cheeks after I'd been gargling your dick and swallowing your sperm half of the night," she replied, smiling sexily.

I was lying in bed, but that didn't stop my knees from becoming weak.

"Jesusss," I groaned.

"We are going to finish what you started, Fabian. Know that," she stated, walking towards the door.

"And that we shall. That we shall."

§§§

Thanks to Cleophus and Santana, Maxon and Angel would be staying at their house for two days. From the jump, Maxon was on board; he loved being around his great-uncle and Santana. I

highly believed Maxon had a small crush on
Santana. Several times, I caught him staring at
her, slobber slipping from the corners of his
mouth. Now, Angel was a different story. She
didn't want to leave her mother's side, but she
quickly changed her mind the moment Cleophus
mentioned a small shopping spree and an
unlimited supply of fun time. The pretty little
one was going to worn out before six o'clock;
there was no doubt in my mind she was going to
sleep like a baby for the rest of the night.

With the kids gone, I sort of felt out of place.
It reverted back to being a quiet place;
thankfully, it wasn't lonely. Two adults in the
house and no children equaled time to get nasty
and have fun with it. Thanks to NaTashia, I
walked around my place naked; that was
something new, and I welcomed it with open
arms. My beautiful one didn't mind prancing
about without an ounce of clothing on. She was
carefree and vibrant. The joy in her eyes and the
smile on her face were priceless.

After we cleaned our house, we chilled in the
front room, reflecting on past years and the
happenings of earlier this morning. Had enough
of talking, I shut her up for a while. The only
sounds coming from her mouth were many

pleasure noises. As our skins slapped, several knocks sounded at the door. We ignored it while we created the most beautiful music. Eventually, whoever received the hint and walked away from our door.

"Whew, shit. It's four o'clock," NaTashia yawned, laying on my chest.

"Yep. You must got something planned?" I asked, running my hand through her thick, natural tresses.

"Grocery shopping. There is minimal food in this joint," she voiced, slowly sliding her hand down my chest.

"We can do that tomorrow. I just want to chill with you. You know I'm all for ordering out."

"See, I'm not for that. I like to cook."

"I know, but can we order out tonight? I don't want to miss a beat with you, especially since the kids are gone," I stated, planting a kiss on her forehead.

"I'll think about it." She smiled, glaring at me.

Cracking a smile, I replied, "Do that."

Silence overcame us as my man grew, resulting in NaTashia purring like a kitten.

Rapidly, she hopped away from me, shaking her head, and saying, "Oh no. We need a break from that."

Sitting upright, I grabbed her wrists and replied, "You been getting on me, not the other way around. So, who are you really trying to convince? It gotta be yourself, Nana."

Looking at my erect man, she whimpered, "Hush up, Fabian."

Wanting another piece of my Nana, I gripped my hardened tool and said, "You want him, don't you?"

Trying to escape the death grip of her wrists, she looked away and laughed. "Fabian, we can do something else. We don't want to exhaust ourselves by having amazing, incredibly awesome sex."

Immediately, I became offended. I didn't see it as us having sex. What I did to her body wasn't sex; it was the art of making love. I was in the process of creating another member to add to our family.

"Get on him," I commanded, squinting my eyes and holding my guy.

"No," she squealed blushing.

"Nana," I called out as she broke free of my grasp.

As she ran towards the kitchen, laughing, I hollered, "Ole childish ass, woman. Come here."

"Nope! You want me? Better, come get me!" she hollered playfully.

"Are we seriously going to play this game, Nana?" I questioned, standing.

She didn't say anything; thus, I asked again. As I walked towards the kitchen, a lone thought came to mind. In our teen days, it was a group of us out and about, chilling in one of the projects. Some kind of way, a game of 'Hide and Seek' came about. All of the females, minus NaTashia, were sought. She had the most disappointing and hurt expression plastered on her oval-shaped face.

I knew what I had to do; the one thing I wanted to do that day, but I refrained from doing so. Quietly, I tiptoed through the kitchen, peeking and seeking for the one I should've sought after instead of Tiffany Langston.

NaTashia wasn't in the kitchen; therefore, I walked towards the bedrooms. She wasn't in any of them or the bathrooms. Strolling towards the front room, I carefully scanned the area. As I observed the furniture, I heard a small scuffle coming from the kitchen. With a smile on my face, I walked towards that way with my dick in my hand.

Playing along with my girl, I said, "Oh, Nana, where you at, woman?"

The only sounds I heard were from the cars and the refrigerator.

"Ohh, Nana, where are you?" I asked, looking around the kitchen and grabbing a mistletoe off the kitchen counter.

Underneath the table, the sexy beauty eyed me as I couldn't tear my eyes away from her.

Still, in play mode, I said, "Now, where did this guh go?"

After bypassing the table, I quickly turned around and slide the chair out of the way. Bending, I ran two of my fingers from the bottom of her feet until I reached her hair.

Sexily, she said, "You found me."

As I tugged on her hair, NaTashia crawled from under the table, looking like an entire fucking meal.

Face to face, I voiced, "Yes, I did find you."

Growling, I parted her lips with my tongue. The sensual, fiery kiss had her moaning in my mouth as my dick grew harder and throbbed.

"I want you inside of me, Fabian," she cooed, ceasing our pink flesh from dancing.

Gripping her hair tighter, I aggressively placed her face down on the four-seat, lemon-scented table and asked, "How bad you want me, Nana?"

Whimpering, she replied, "Real, real, real bad, Fabian."

"Is that so?" I responded, slowly spreading her legs.

"Yess."

Biting my bottom lip, I lifted her butt cheeks. While I rubbed the head of my dick against her wet folds, NaTashia's body trembled, causing me to groan. Her nails scraped the table; my toes curled. The heat from her pussy had me dying to be inside; yet, I refrained from doing so. I wanted to see how impatient she would become if I didn't give her what she wanted.

While I teased and taunted the beauty of all beauties, she purred and whined.

A few minutes into my agonizing game, NaTashia whipped her hand around as if she was possessed and hollered, "Sometime to-fucking-day, Fabian!"

Laughing, I pressed her head down and shoved my guy inside of its home.

"Shit, Fabian!" she seductively screamed as I drove my dick in every corner of her festive pussy.

It was a no-brainer how NaTashia wanted the dick. She had witnessed me in action plenty of times; she wanted a sample of the hood nigga in me. Thus, I gave her a little taste of it; after all, I wasn't up for bruising her cervix as I'd done the others. I didn't want her to be sore days upon days.

"This what you want, Nana?" I voiced, beating that juicy thing up as I danced in it.

With an uncontrollably shaking body, she nodded and said, "Yessss."

Long, deep stroking the kitty, I asked, "Did he fuck you like this?"

Rapidly, shaking her head, she oddly voiced, "Nothing like thisss."

In need of getting deeper into her lovely kitty, I bent my knees, all the while pulling her hair. Growled, I asked, "Then why you ain't bring your motherfucking ass back home to the one who could've been fucking, sexing, and making love to you like this? Why you kept letting that nigga play around with this pussy, knowing damn well he wasn't certified enough to take care of it?"

I wasn't looking for an answer; I wanted her to think about it; therefore, I drilled her petite body. With every deep thrust, my anger and frustration escaped me. She loved it; her pleasure noises told me so. No matter the speed I served my loving, NaTashia caught it.

Every slap to the ass and thighs, she took it like a woman. Apparently, she needed wanted to be punished just as much as I had to punish her.

I noticed she had a deep arch in her back and standing on her tiptoes. To me, that was a clear indication I was a little too rough with my Nana. Therefore, I started to slowly stroke her kitty.

"Fabiannn!" she hollered before saying, "I'm cumming!"

"Handle that shit, Nana," I growled, still angry with her.

"Oouuahh!" she moaned. Her body shook and leaned inwards. Before long, NaTashia's body was going to lock, and I was going to beat her G-Spot up, for the old and new.

Through clenched teeth, I said, "That late evening in the hood, I saw you … hiding inside of Mr. Rogers shed. I saw you, Nana. Badly, I wanted to come in with you, but I was afraid of doing so."

"I know you saw me, Fabian. I saw you looking at me, but instead, you went to Tiffany," she replied, body stuck to the table.

"I ... I wanted to do this to you ...," I stated, closing in on her.

Latching my mouth onto hers, I sucked her tongue and drove my dick in and out of her wet fortress, all the while spreading her ass cheeks.

"Fuck! Fabiannn Wellsss!" she screamed, gripping the back of my head and glaring into my eyes.

"I so badly wanted to do this to you, that day and many days before and after that. I'm sorry I didn't. I'm sorry the kids aren't mine, biologically. I'm sorry I didn't come after you, Nana. I'm sorry I left you behind. I regret never coming after you during that game. I regret I never fought for you to stay here after graduation. I was a pussy ass nigga for letting you leave and staying gone," I softly stated, watching the tears fall from her eyes.

Weakly, she asked, "Did any of them mean anything to you?"

Shaking my head, I truthfully said, "Not a single one. It was always you, Nana. Always you."

Those beautiful tears of hers cascaded down her face as she gently whined, "Cum in me, Fabian."

Those were some beautiful words; words I had been waiting for her to say, even though I had been nutting in her since last night.

"I'm going to do that regardless, but I'm not ready yet. I'll let you know when so we can cum together," I voiced as my phone rang.

While we continued handling our business, my phone stopped ringing, only to ring again. By the tenth time my phone rang, I knew it was an important call. I didn't want to get out of NaTashia's fortress, and I sure as hell didn't want to miss that phone call. The only thing I knew to do was carry her into the front room, shoving dick into her pussy as I walked.

"Ooouu, Fabian. What the hell?" she asked in a shocked but turned on manner.

"I gotta answer this call, but I refuse to stop what we got going on," I groaned as her pretty pink muscles clenched my guy.

While I reached for my cell phone, NaTashia beautifully moaned as she placed her knees and hands on the sofa.

"You take that phone call, and I'll handle him," she voiced as I saw Cleophus' name and the many missed calls from him.

"Um, you might want to put that on hold. It was Cleophus calling," I replied as I returned my partner's call.

Eyeing me and working her pretty kitty on my guy, she replied, "Like hell I am."

"Damn, 'bout time I hear yo' voice nigga. OG Buckingham is dead," Cleophus stated while NaTashia bounced up and down on my guy.

I tried to sound normal as I asked, "What happened?"

"His wife found him inside of their bathroom, dead."

"Damn, that's fucked up. It ain't a suspicious knock-off, is it?" I asked, tapping on NaTashia's booty, all the while slowly thrusting my guy inside of her.

Looking back at me, she smiled and seductively bit her bottom lip. For a split second, I forgot I was on the phone. It was Cleophus's statement that reminded me.

"In an hour, we have a meetin' wit' OG Buckingham right-hand nigga, OG Mag."

With a frown on my face, I asked, "For what? We don't run with them niggas like that."

"Since his partner in crime is gone, the old man steppin' down. Accordin' to OG Mag, he an' OG Buckingham been lookin' at you an' me fo' a while to take over there shit," he voiced, sounding exhausted.

Not liking the idea, I expressed that to my homie. I didn't like how the young ones moved. They were too flashy and talkative for me. I didn't want any parts of that crew. They would be murdered fucking around with me.

"Well, we will have to express this to OG Mag. I'll be there to pick you up in thirty minutes. So, be ready nigga," he voiced while exhaling what I knew was weed smoke.

Disappointed that I had to leave my girl, I replied, "A'ight."

Thinking of the kids, I hollered, "Aye, what our kids doing?"

Laughing, he said, "Shid, Angel knocked out. I wore her ass out. She thought she could hang wit' me. Took them to that trampoline park. That took her out the game an' almost landed me in the hospital. A nigga limpin' an' shit. Maxon, ole slick self, underneath Santana like he's a newborn baby."

Throughout the entire time, my partner talked, NaTashia's pussy had me weak at the knees. Between the heat coming and an unlimited supply of wetness had me lowly growling and gripping that rounded ass of hers.

"Bitch, I know you ain't fuckin' my niece while on the phone wit' me?" Cleophus laughed.

More like your niece fucking me while I'm on the phone with you, I thought as I struggled to say, "I'll be ready in thirty minutes. Don't come early and don't come late, either."

"Bet, ole tender dick ass nigga!" he loudly announced before ending the call.

"So, I guess we need to finish this before your time is up, right?" NaTashia asked as I dropped my phone on the ground.

"Yeah. Some business we need to handle," I replied as I matched her thrust.

"Okay."

I didn't want to change the beat of our song, but I had to. I wasn't going to leave her unsatisfied. By the time we reached the end of our long song, my abdomen region was wet and not from sweat. NaTashia had a super soaker; so fucking wet, her juices dripped out of her like a water faucet on high mode.

As I poorly rested against the sofa, she softly whined.

"I'm going to carry you into the bathroom. You ready?"

Slowly, she nodded. Before we sauntered down the hallway, I picked up my cell phone, and

NaTashia rested her head on my shoulders, arms wrapped around my neck. Before I made it to our room, my cell phone rang. Sighing deeply, I glared at my phone and saw Auntie Rebecca's name.

On the fourth ring, I answered.

"Hello there, Nephew," she spoke calmly.

"Hi, Auntie. I heard about OG Buckingham. I'm sorry for your loss," I told her as I stepped into my room.

"Thank you, Sweet face," she stated before saying, "I'm at your front door. I need to talk to you. Will you let me in?"

Stunned, I replied, "Yeah. I'll be right there."

"Okay," she voiced before we ended the call.

Placing NaTashia in the bathroom, I said, "One of my mother's estranged sister's is at the door. I'm going to see what she wants. You can shower without me."

"Okay," she yawned, sauntering towards the tub.

Before I exited the bathroom, I washed my face and pondered should I put on my robe or throw on some lounging clothes. It didn't take long for me to decide to throw on a pair of jogging pants and dash towards the front door.

Upon opening it, I glared into my auntie's beautiful, dark-skinned face and said, "I'm sorry for having you wait so long. Please come in."

As she stepped across the door's threshold, she cracked a smile and said, "I have been in your driveway for a while."

Closing the door behind me, I asked in a puzzled manner, "Why?"

"Let's just say I heard what was going on in here from the driveway. I wouldn't want to be disturbed, so I didn't bother you and your lady friend. Um, speaking of lady friend ... where is she?"

"Taking a shower," I voiced, smiling from ear to ear.

"Good," she quickly stated before asking, "Is there somewhere we can talk privately?"

"Yes, I have a man cave. Would you like anything to drink?"

"No, thank you," she replied, glaring into my face.

Auntie Rebecca's light brown peepers showed a flicker of sadness. There was no need to ask what was wrong. Upon our first meet and greet, she told me I reminded her so much of her dear sister.

Leading the way towards my chill room, I pondered what my auntie wanted to speak about. I hoped it wasn't anything that'll cause me to hurt her feelings, but in a polite way.

As I closed the door, she cleared her throat and said, "Nephew, my sweet-faced nephew."

"Ma'am?" I voiced, taking a seat next to her.

"Thirty-seven years ago, the worst type of thing any man could do to a woman was done. That type of hurt causes unwanted things to happen. I'm the definition of loyal. It doesn't get any realer than me. Understand what I'm saying?"

Even though I partially understood what she said, I still nodded.

"You see, I helped that motherfucka become a powerful bastard. It was my resources, my intellect, my aggressiveness, and of course, my sex appeal to grant him half of the shit he accomplished during his lifetime. Willie was nothing without me," she ranted.

As my auntie continued venting about her late husband, I listened actively, wondering why she would choose to tell me everything. Then, it became clear. She knew about his affair thirty seven years ago. Instantly, I paid attention to her body language.

Did she know who NaTashia was? Is she here to kill her?

"Willie slept with a woman, producing a child. This particular child is to inherit everything. The cars, large amounts of money, two large apartment complexes out of town, and every iron dime of his life insurance policy minus the amount it takes to bury his funky ass," she bluntly spoke, glaring into my face.

"How do you know?"

"I saw some papers hidden in his gentleman only room. He didn't leave any of our six children anything. He left it all to this nameless child."

Shit, I thought as I asked, "Auntie, I don't mean to be rude, but what are you trying to ask of me or tell me."

"I want to know who the child is, and I want you to find him or her."

"Okay," I voiced before asking, "Do you know who the person's mother is?"

Shaking her head, she replied, "Nope."

Thank God, I thought as I questioned, "Have you asked any of OG Buckingham's close associates?"

"Tuh, they would never tell me anything. They sure as hell ain't going to tell you. They will die before they leak that key information."

"I have to ask," I spoke before continuing, "What are your plans for said child?"

"I want to know what's so special about *this* one than the ones we made together. I need to know does he or she remembers my husband, and if so, did he love her mother," my auntie stated firmly, yet her eyes shown she was hurt.

Clearing my throat, I asked, "To be clear, you don't want said child's head on a spike?"

Rapidly shaking her head, Auntie Rebecca replied, "No. That child isn't the cause of my late husband's treachery. That child owes me nothing but a few answers."

Nodding, I said, "Auntie, I'm going to be real with you ... I need more information about the child, like the exact date of birth and where he or she was born. That's not just half of it. I really need concrete information to begin this search. If not, we are looking at a dead end. That's until he or she comes forward and claims everything OG Buckingham left."

"See, I don't want to wait until the child claims anything. I want my answers now. He sure as hell couldn't answer before I tased him while he was on the toilet."

Repeatedly and quickly, I blinked my eyes and said, "Come again?"

"Sweet face, you heard me."

Lowly, I asked, "Auntie, did you murder your husband?"

With a smile on her face, she shook her head and replied, "No, Sweet face, why would I do such a thing, knowing he had heart problems already?"

Knock. Knock. Knock.

Shortly after the soft knocks, NaTashia asked, "Fabian, I'm going to the store. Do you mind if I take Bessie?"

In need of getting her far away from my auntie, I replied, "Yes."

"Okay. Is there anything you would like for me to get while I'm out?"

"A case of bottled water."

"Okay. I'll be back soon as I can."

"Be careful, baby," I said, looking towards the door.

"I will," she responded.

At the same time, Auntie Rebecca placed her hand on top of mine and happily stated, "I would love to meet her. Tell her to come inside."

Thank God she doesn't know what the child looks like or the child's name, I thought as I called out to NaTashia.

"Yes?" she loudly said, sounding as if she was close to the garage door.

"Can you come in and meet my auntie, please?"

"Sure thing," she excitedly replied as I heard the garage door close.

"She must be something special if you allowing her to drive Bessie," Auntie Rebecca voiced, glaring into my face.

Looking into her eyes, I responded, "More than you'll ever know. I'll blow a motherfucker brains out about her."

As I watched my auntie's facial expression, the door opened.

"Hey," NaTashia beautifully voiced, stepping into our line of vision.

My auntie stood, shocked and shaking. The color in her face drained as she couldn't tear her eyes away from NaTashia.

Immediately, I stood and asked, "Auntie, are you all right?"

Weakly, my auntie said, "Yes, I'm all right, Sweet face."

Extending her hand, NaTashia said, "I'm NaTashia. It's nice to meet you."

It was a while before my auntie placed her hand into NaTashia's soft palm. My auntie didn't let NaTashia's hand go; my girl had to pry her hand away.

Immediately, I became alarmed.

There's no way she could know who NaTashia's father is. She doesn't know the child's name or what the child looks like; she said so herself . . . unless she lied to me, I thought as I cleared my throat.

Wiping a tear from her face, Auntie Rebecca said, "That's why you are his prized possession. That's why he's left you everything."

Oh fuck.

Oddly smiling, NaTashia looked at me before placing her eyes on my auntie and said, "Um, forgive me. I'm not understanding."

"Your father. My late husband. He's left you everything minus the house we built together and the cars I own," my auntie stated, on the verge of crying.

Lightly chuckling, NaTashia said, "Ma'am, maybe you have me mistaken for someone else. I'm sorry for your loss."

OG Buckingham's death isn't a loss to her, I thought as Auntie Rebecca said, "Willie Buckingham is your father. I never knew of you until he passed away and I found some papers. Technically, I didn't know of you. Upon placing my eyes on you ... I know just who you are. You are my husband's love-child. You look just like his mother. From her healthy, beautiful mane down to her average-sized feet. You are built just like her. Have her smile and all. The resemblance is uncanny."

Stunned out of my mind, I had to do some probing of my own. Seeing my auntie wasn't a threat to NaTashia, I asked questions my girl couldn't. I wanted to know about this mother of OG Buckingham and why she felt NaTashia was his prized possession. Auntie Rebecca didn't answer a single question until NaTashia sat across from us.

"I'm going to make this long story a short one. On his twelfth birthday, Willie and his mother visited family and friends in their home state, Mississippi. While they were out and about, walking, a group of White men was acting suspiciously. So, his mother told him to go back to their family's house. He didn't. Instead, he hid. Willie watched those men rape and murder his mother. You see, Willie loved his mother something awful. He wanted to die for her, but

being the strong and loving mother she was ...
she had forbidden it. She wanted her son to live a
productive life ... for her. He was a momma's
boy. Every holiday, birthday, and death
anniversary, he visited his mother's grave in
Mississippi. On her birthday and death date, he
would host a huge party in her honor. NaTashia
is his prized possession because she's the spitting
image of the one woman he loved more than any
woman in this world, including me," she stated
softly, eyeing NaTashia.

Silence overcame the room. There wasn't
anything either of us could say as Auntie Rebecca
continued to glare at my woman.

Breaking the silence, NaTashia said, "You
stated something about me inheriting some
things from him?"

Nodding her head, Auntie Rebecca curtly
replied, "Correct."

Standing, NaTashia said, "I don't want
anything he's left me. Keep it for yourself and
y'all's kids. After all, it's not like I knew him. My
entire existence is the reason why my life was
pure hell and then some. Please point me in the
right direction so I can sign everything over to
you, ma'am."

Stunned at my baby's answer, Auntie Rebecca said, "You don't want to know what he's left you."

Shaking her head, NaTashia replied, "No. I wasn't the one in his life. I shouldn't be the one getting it all. It's not fair to those that were there. As my mother likes to say, 'I was just the unwanted bastard child from a naïve woman and a smooth-talking man'."

Hearing the hurt in NaTashia's voice, I paid close attention to her. She was ready to go, most likely to poke the hornet's nest.

"NaTashia," Auntie Rebecca gently called.

"Yes?"

"Did your mother really tell you that?"

"And plenty more shit to go along with it. It was nice meeting you," NaTashia rapidly stated to my auntie.

"Likewise," Auntie Rebecca replied in a sad tone.

Placing her eyes on me, NaTashia asked, "Are you sure you don't have any special request for our late dinner?"

Shaking my head, I replied, "No, baby, whatever you cook ... trust, I'm eating."

"Okay," she voiced, walking towards me.

After placing a kiss on my lips, I noticed the tears welling in her eyes.

"I'll walk you to Bessie," I told her.

Waving her hand, she said, "I'm okay. I promise you I'm okay."

"I love you, Nana."

"I love you more, Fabo," she voiced before walking out of the door.

Silence overcame us until I heard the speakers of Bessie. NaTashia was in her feelings, and I didn't like that.

"Nephew, what kind of mother tells her child ... she carried for nine months ... some shit like that?" Auntie Rebecca asked sadly.

Sighing heavily, I glared into my auntie's eyes and said, "A bitter, heartless, and cruel bitch."

Chapter Nine

NaTashia

For years, I wondered who my father was. Often, I swore he couldn't have known I existed because he wouldn't let me suffer in my mother's hellish house. Hearing that man of a father left me money and other materialistic things pissed me off. He knew who I was, and he didn't save me. To hell with him and his materialistic shit! Money and the other items weren't going to pacify the suffering I had been through with my mother. It wasn't going to halfway makeup for being told I wasn't worthy enough to have a life like most kids, teenagers.

I had every intention of going grocery shopping, but I put it on hold as I drove to my mother's house. That broad had some explaining to do, or it could've been I wanted to curse her ass out. I was frustrated, and the only person I knew to take it out on was the woman who had given birth to me.

Arriving at her house, I shut off the engine and hurriedly exited Bessie. Upon walking towards the front door, it opened; Momma stood there, glaring at me as if I was stank.

"What do you want?" she inquired, looking me up and down.

"Does the name Willie Buckingham ring a bell?" I asked, inches away from her.

Those evil, medium-beaded, brown eyes of hers fluttered. Looking at the ground, her shoulders relaxed as she sighed heavily. It was apparent her mind went into the past. I didn't have time for her to have a closed mouth. I needed answers.

Loudly, I asked, "Does Willie Buckingham's motherfucking name ring a bell, Momma?"

Placing her eyes on me, she softly said, "Yes."

"Who is he to me?" I questioned, stepping closer to her.

She didn't respond. Thus, I asked, "Well, who was he to you?"

Exhaling sharply, Momma said, "He's your father, NaTashia. I loved him, and he didn't love me. Is there anything else you want to know?"

"Plenty," I shot back before continuing, "It was apparent he knew about me since he left me some things. Now, tell me why you never told me who he was or why I never saw him? Why would a man leave a child so much wealth, but she doesn't know him?"

"Wealth. What do you mean?" she asked, eyes lightening up.

"Don't worry about what he left me. Answer the questions, I spit out."

"Maybe we need to sit down and have this talk," she softly voiced.

Shaking my head, I replied, "No, I'm good. So, spill because I have some shit I need to do."

"You don't have to talk to me like that, NaTashia," she stated, eyes teary.

Softly laughing, I said, "Momma, please stop that. You don't give a damn about me. Why worry about the way I speak to you? To be respected, you have to give it. Now, can we get on with this talk?"

Nodding her head, she asked, "How did you find out that he's your father?"

"His wife."

Momma's knees buckled as she clutched her chest.

"What do you mean?" Momma inquired as she zoned out, thinking.

"Willie's wife is Fabian's auntie. She wanted to meet me. She froze when she saw me. She stated I looked just like his mother, and that's when I learned who's partially responsible for me having a hellish life."

With a gentle smile on her face, Momma said, "That's what he told me upon seeing you after I had you. He had the biggest smile on his face as he held you and planted many kisses on your feet, hands, and face. Willie fell in love with you at first sight. It was amazing to see a man who was known for selling more drugs than a pharmacy. I gave you your first name, and Willie named you Marie … after his mother."

"Oh, ain't that nice," I replied in a sullen tone, rolling my eyes.

Quickly, Momma asked in a frightened manner, "Does she know who I am?"

"Not that I'm aware of. Why?"

"Let's just say that Rebecca is one powerful female outside of your father."

Laughing, I replied, "That's absurd. That woman doesn't look anything like a gangster woman. She's clean-cut and proper."

"That's what she wants everyone to think. Anyways, are you sure she doesn't know who I am?"

Shrugging, I said, "I don't know. Maybe she and Fabian discussed me more after I left. Now, to the questions I asked you. Answer them. I'm pressed for time."

"What were the questions, again?" Momma voiced, gazing at me.

"Why you never told me who he was or why I never saw him? Why would a man leave a child so much wealth, but she doesn't know him?"

"You never saw him because I kept you away from him."

"Why?"

"Because he hit me more than once. There was no way I was going to allow you to be around a woman beater," she voiced, tearing her eyes away.

"Why did he hit you?" I probed.

She wasn't quick to offer up an answer, so I rattled some off.

"Was it because you were mean to me? Did you abuse me? Did you mistreat me at an early age, Momma?"

Tears streamed down her face as she said, "I hated you. He only loved you. He only came over to see you. He only did for you. We constantly argued about how he treated me versus how he treated you. I didn't like it one bit. I took him away from you because he failed to love me. I told him that if he tried to see you again, I would ensure he would spend the rest of his life in prison. He left you wealth because out of all of his children, you were his favorite. You were his world, all because of your looks."

I couldn't be stunned or shocked at her answers. After all, Momma had been stopped surprising me by the words that escaped her mouth. She was indeed a bitter old woman who was going to die that way.

Shaking my head, I asked, "To be clear, I've never disappointed you. You hated me with everything in you because of Willie Buckingham's loving nature towards me. Is that about right?"

Silence overcame us as a car zoomed down the road.

Backing away, I said, "Your ways towards me is the reason why your other siblings don't have anything to do with you, huh?"

"I'm done answering questions, NaTashia," she voiced as the next-door neighbor stepped onto his porch.

"I'm done asking them. Enjoy your miserable ass life, woman. You are truly missing out," I stated before turning around and walking towards the car.

As I opened the door, she asked, "Did Rebecca say how he died? When is his funeral or viewing of his body, NaTashia?"

Hopping in the car, my cell phone rang. While I retrieved my device, Momma was walking to the car, yelling the same questions she asked before I sat in the car.

"Hello," I said into the phone as I started the engine.

"Where are you?" Cleophus asked as I dropped the gearshift into the reverse position.

"Leaving your sister's house."

"Fabian told me that you learned who your father is. How do you feel about that?"

Zooming off my mother's driveway, I said, "I don't feel any kind of way. I didn't know the man."

Sighing sharply, Cleophus said, "He loved you more than you would ever know."

"And how would you know that, Cleophus?"

"Because he took pleasure in telling me that every time I saw him, which was daily. Don't think for a second he didn't know anything about you. He did. He appointed me to be your protector, even though I was going to be that anyway. He ensured I stayed out of harm's way so I could protect and care for you. When we hopped into our teenage years, OG Buckingham ensured I had money in my pockets. Once Fabian stood by my side, OG Buckingham made sure to give us a couple more hundred dollars for you. Yes, he knew of Fabian's feelings for you. Anyways, OG Buckingham made sure you enjoyed life just as much as any other child did, NaTashia. I have some letters from him that belong to you. When you turned twelve, he started writing to you. At first, he wanted me to give them to you, but he changed his mind. He made it clear that I wasn't to give you the letters until he died. When Fabian and I come back from this meeting, I will give the letters to you and answer any questions. Okay?"

Nodding, I replied, "Okay."

"I'll see you once the meetings over, Nana."

"All right," I voiced, ending the call.

I wasn't a ball of confusion, nor was I frustrated. I was at peace of knowing why my mother hated me so much. Finally, I knew who fathered me. I no longer had to ponder about anything.

Arriving at an expensive yet quality food store parking lot, my cell phone rang. On the third ring, I answered the call from Fabian.

"Hello," I stated as I parked Bessie.

"What you doing, sexy woman?"

Smiling, I said, "Getting ready to grocery shop."

"Have fun," he stated, exhaling.

"That I will do."

"You exited the house in a hurry and wouldn't let me walk you to the garage. So, I didn't get a chance to make sure you were okay. Nana, tell me how you are really feeling?" he inquired lovingly.

"Honestly, I'm fine. Like I said before, I didn't know the man well enough to feel pressed by his passing or the fact my mother slept with a married man and kept him away from me because he wouldn't love her. The truth is out. At least I know who the other party is that's responsible for my creation."

As I shut off the engine and opened the door, Fabian said, "My auntie likes you, Nana. She wants to get to know you better."

If I wasn't shocked by anything I learned today, I surely was stunned by Rebecca wanting to get to know me. In my eyes, it was strange for her to want to know more about her husband's bastard child.

"Hello," Fabian stated.

"I'm here," I said, stepping out of the car.

"Thought I lost you there for a minute."

Shaking my head, I voiced, "I'm here, just stunned, that's all."

"Why?"

"The situation."

"I'm not. Who wouldn't want to get to know you? You are something exceptional and rare. She would be stupid not to get to know the woman who has her nephew's heart in a chokehold."

"Hm," I sounded off, walking towards the food store.

"Seeing that you only have a select few words to say, I'm going to let you get on with your shopping. Once I make it back to the house, after you and Cleophus talk, you and I will have a chit chat as well."

"All right."

"I love you, Nana."

"I love you, Fabian," I replied before we ended the call.

Zipping inside the chilly grocery store, I focused on what I wanted to prepare for dinner. After grabbing a shopping cart, I retrieved a few recipes from the rack closest to the entrance doors. While making my way through the store, I thought of how Rebecca must've felt knowing her husband cheated and created another life. Instantly, I felt empathy for the woman. Once again, I was on the receiving end of a cheating man with another family.

I wonder is that why Fabian kept asking me about how I felt, I thought as I placed a bag of apples into the cart.

The more I shopped, the more I felt down. It seemed as if my existence brought pain to those I never knew about. I didn't like it one bit. How was I supposed to look into Rebecca's eyes or be around her knowing how I was conceived? How was I supposed to get to know a woman when I didn't know how she truly felt about me?

"So, it's true, he does have another child? Is it a girl or boy?" a high-pitched tone woman said.

"A girl," a familiar voiced woman replied.

Slowing my pace, I listened actively to Rebecca and the unknown person's conversation.

"What does she look like? What's her name? I hope you are not planning on letting her get a dime of our father's money or an ounce of property. I don't care if he left it to her. You are his wife, Momma; isn't there anything you can do to keep her from getting what is rightfully ours?" Rebecca's daughter stated.

That was my cue to deaden the conversation while they were at a public place. Plus, I needed a few items off the canned goods aisle.

As graceful as she was inside of Fabian's home, his auntie was the same way, shoulders and head held high. The woman was well-composed as she glared into her daughter's long, oval-shaped, dark-hued face.

I had the need to say something in my defense; yet, I refrained from doing so. There was no need in me repeating myself twice to a woman I didn't know. I was clear when I told her I didn't want anything he had left me.

Upon me bypassing them, Rebecca called my name. For a split second, I thought of carrying on as if I didn't hear her. Yet, I turned around and glared into their faces.

"I would like you to meet someone," Rebecca stated with a smile on her face. Her daughter's mouth dropped as she couldn't tear her eyes away from me.

Shaking my head, I voiced, "If you aren't going to introduce me as Fabian's girlfriend, then there isn't a need for any introduction."

"Momma, I know this isn't Daddy's other child, the *one* that's going to get everything. She looks just like Grandma Marie," the spoiled bitch stated, glaring at her mother.

"Monique, she doesn't want any of it."

"And how do you know that?" Monique voiced, glancing at me.

Before Rebecca had the chance to speak, I said, "Because I told her today, I don't want it. Also, I told her if there are any papers I need to sign stating I don't want any of it… she knows where to find me."

As I turned on my heels, Rebecca gently called my name.

"Yes?" I replied, giving her my undivided attention.

"I don't blame you for my husband's infidelity. The blame isn't anywhere near you. Yes, I'm upset he left our children out of his final wishes, but I do not hate or wish ill on you. I hope you believe me," she sincerely spoke.

I didn't say anything as I nodded.

"I do think you should get to know your siblings and father's side of the family," Rebecca stated.

"Speak for yourself, Momma. I hope you don't think I've grown enough to accept someone he was willing to give his all to and not think of us. I'm not that damn mature," Monique spat, looking at me as if I smelled bad.

Chuckling and shaking my head, I replied to Rebecca, "That's a lovely gesture, but I will decline on that. I went all of my life not knowing him and his family. I'm fine not getting to know anyone. I don't have time for snide comments and hatred from people I don't know, and honestly, I care less to get to know anyone. It does lift the weight off my shoulders, knowing the man's name who aided in giving me life. I will have a name to tell my children, so they know their lineage. As far as I'm concerned, that's good enough. That's all I ever wanted."

Nodding, she said, "This situation is very unique and tender to the heart. Yes, your father was my husband, but I am Fabian's auntie. My children, your siblings, are his cousins. At some point, we will be in a room together. We will be in each other's lives, NaTashia."

"This is the one Fabian's crazy about? This is Nana?" Monique inquired, shocked.

Ignoring the cunt, I replied, "And for Fabian's sake, I will be present with a smile on my face."

"That's all I can ask for," Rebecca calmly stated as Monique's cell phone rang.

"Have a good day, Rebecca," I said, turning around.

As her daughter yapped on the phone, talking about me, Rebecca said, "I'm so sorry for everything you endured growing up, NaTashia. A mother should never treat or talk to her child as if she's nothing."

"What she endured? What her momma said to her? Who is her momma? Do we know her?" Monique inquired as I came to a halt.

What in the fuck did Fabian tell his auntie? I thought as Rebecca didn't answer her daughter's probing question.

Prancing away, I felt their eyes on me. I was burning up inside. I wanted to ring Fabian's fucking neck. He had no right to speak of my mother's and my relationship. That was my fucking business, not his gotdamn auntie's.

While I aggressively and quickly grocery shopped, I couldn't wait until Fabian was in my face. I was going to lay his ass out. He had the game fucked up, discussing me with his auntie. In all of our years of being friends, I had never cursed him out, but today I was going to blow his motherfucking scalp back with what I had to say. He had crossed a major line, and he was going to know never to do that shit again!

Chapter Ten

Fabian

"Don't tell me you are really thinking about us taking over OG Buckingham's crew?" I asked Cleophus soon as we took a seat in his car.

Looking at me, he asked, "Why not?"

"Because I don't want more shit on my plate than I already have. We are comfortable, dude. We have been blessed to stay out of prison and other shit. We always said we weren't going to deal with a large crew. Why would we start now?"

"Because I want to be bigger than I am. Don't you?"

"Fuck no. I don't want an army behind us. We handle shit just fine. Those young niggas don't know how to act. I don't have the patience or time to be dealing with egos and pride. Did you see how Orthello looked at us and then OG Mag when he stated who he wanted to run the crew? Keep in mind, Orthello is my cousin."

"Yeah, I saw that shit," he voiced, starting the engine.

"That's blood, nigga, and by his looks that nigga ready for a war. I'm sure he thought he was going to be over the crew. Blood will be shed, not from us if we take over that crew. I'm the type of nigga that'll knock family off if they come to me the wrong way. I don't want to step on nobody's toes; I hate to be standing beside my auntie while she buries another loved one. I'm going to tell you like this, Cleophus, I don't want any parts in OG Buckingham crew, and I stand on that shit."

Reversing out of the yard, Cleophus nodded his head and said, "I heard you the first time, nigga."

"Hearing and understanding me are two different things. If you pursue this shit, I have to respectfully bow out. There won't be any hard feelings towards us. Just know that," I told him as I glared into his face.

"I'mma hold you to that, Fabian," he sighed, zooming down the road.

At that moment, I knew what my best friend was going to do. As soon as he talked to NaTashia, he would find him another right-hand man and set up plays to take over the most massive crew in the city.

The ride to my house was quiet. I didn't see the need to spark up a conversation; I left my friend alone with his thoughts as I dipped into my own thinking.

Ever since I started hustling, I had always saved money. I was a teenager, living in my parents' house; it wasn't like I had any bills. Momma was still buying clothes and shoes for me; with my lawn care money, I took care of my grooming and whatever Bessie needed. Thankful for the lawn care hustle, it masked what I was really doing in the streets with Cleophus. I was the one who told him he needed to find a gig to conceal what he was doing. If it wasn't for me, Cleophus would've been fucked up a long time ago. He wasn't a thinker like me; he was all action and deal with the consequences later type of dude. Becoming the head honcho of a large group of rowdy niggas was not a good thing for him if I wasn't to his right.

"What are you thinkin' 'bout?" Cleophus asked, pulling into my driveway.

"How big of a mistake you are going to make if you take on something so big without me being by your side," I said, looking at him.

"Then, rethink yo' position of sittin' on the sidelines."

Sighing deeply, I responded, "I told you I never wanted to be this big to begin with. The goal was to do this shit long enough for Nana's sake. That's it. We have accrued so much. Why can't you be satisfied with what we have? Honestly, we are blessed to be in this game as long as we have been. Do you know many niggas in the game don't make it to our age? They get too greedy, and shit goes left from there. We are solid because we are loyal to each other. Those niggas don't know shit about loyalty. They are fucking snitches with racks of money. I'm not rethinking my stance on the matter. You should be the one rethinking. If I'm not on your right, shit will go to the left really fucking fast, Cleophus."

"A'ight, man," he quickly voiced, waving me off and opening the door.

I needed my best friend to understand the severity of the things.

Before stepping out of the car, Cleophus grabbed a Nike shoebox and said, "I never thought you, of all people, would give a fuck 'bout the next nigga. I never thought you would step down from somethin' you are fuckin' good at doing."

"I'm thinking of the future, and so far, if we head down the road OG Mag wants us to … it's not going to end well. I'm very sure we won't be six-feet deep, but those that share the same DNA as me will," I voiced as we walked towards the front door.

Before he could open his mouth, NaTashia aggressively yanked open the door. Instantly, my stomach growled as my mouth salivated. The aroma from within the house had me eager to sit at the table and eat.

"What's up, beautiful?" I smiled.

Pointing her finger at me, she said, "Get your black ass in the house. I have a fucking bone to pick with you."

With a straight face, Cleophus said, "Damn nigga, you already in the doghouse. Shit, this show finna be good. I never thought she would ever cuss yo' ass out."

As she walked backward, eyes on me, I stepped across the door's threshold, asking, "What I did?"

"Who told you to run your motherfucking mouth about my life with my mother? That isn't any of your auntie's business, nigga. Let that be the last time you tell her anything about me and my mother, Fabian!" she angrily shouted as Cleophus sat on the couch, glaring at us.

Dumbfounded, I probed, "What are you talking about, Nana? I didn't tell my auntie shit about you and Glorianna. You know damn well I don't have loose lips."

Quickly, she began to tell me what happened at the grocery store. Sighing heavily, I said, "You mentioned to her what your mother had said about an unwanted bastard child from a naïve woman and a smooth-talking man. After you left, Auntie Rebecca asked me what kind of mother tells her child some shit like that. My response was 'a bitter, cruel, and miserable bitch'. After my comment, we didn't discuss anything pertaining to you and Glorianna."

"Mmhm," she spat before walking away.

Not liking the fact she didn't believe me, I hollered, "NaTashia, don't you walk away from me like I'm lying to you! You know I won't lie to you about shit!"

"Okay, Fabian," she stated, disappearing into the kitchen.

As Cleophus's cell phone rang, I sauntered into the great smelling kitchen. While my homie stepped out of the house, yapping his mouth, I wrapped my arms around NaTashia's waist, planted my head in the crook of her neck, and inhaled deeply.

"I'm sorry for accusing you of talking when it was me who set myself up," she softly voiced, placing the large, black spoon on the utensil holder.

"Apology accepted," I replied, planting kisses on her neck.

"I hope you like homemade chicken and shrimp, Parmesan and Asiago cheese fettuccini alfredo. Also, I made a Caesar salad with those little tomatoes you like. Yes, I added green tomatoes and banana peppers. For dessert, Dutch apple pie and pecan and praline ice cream."

Excited as hell to tear into everything she prepared for us, I screeched, "Yeaaahhhh. Nigga going to eat well before and while in bed."

As she laughed, Cleophus stepped into the kitchen and rapidly said, "Nana, here's the letters from OG Buckingham. Do you have any questions fo' me?"

Looking at her uncle, NaTashia replied, "Since I hear the rush in your voice, I'm going to say no, I don't have any questions. If I do, I will wait until you have time to answer them."

"Are you upset with me because I didn't tell you he was your dad?"

Shaking her head, she replied, "Nope."

"You promise?" he asked, holding out his pinky finger.

With a soft smile on her face, NaTashia nodded and voiced, "Yes, I promise."

After they shook pinkies, Cleophus nodded his head and said, "I'mma holla at y'all later. NaTashia, I'll bring the kids som' time tomorrow evening. It won't be too late. I know you have to get them setup fo' school an' shit."

"Okay."

I knew my partner was on another level with me when we didn't dap like we usually did.

When he arrived at the door, I loudly stated, "So, we like that, Cleophus? I voiced my opinion on something, and you act like I'm against you."

"The way I see it, Fabian, you are," he responded, not looking at me.

Becoming angry, I replied, "Face me nigga, like a fucking man, and say that shit ... so I know it's real and not you acting like a spoiled little bitch."

Chuckling, not in a pleasant way, Cleophus said, "No need to face you. You know where I stand on the matter."

Just like that, my male best friend in the entire world walked out of my house as if we didn't have so much history together. Feeling the weight of the world on my shoulders, I tried my best not to drop my head while taking a seat at the table.

"What's going on between y'all, Fabian? Never have I ever seen y'all not dap each other," NaTashia asked, stooping in front of me.

Sighing deeply, I rubbed her face and said, "OG Mag wants us to run OG Buckingham's crew. I don't want any parts of that; whereas, your uncle does. I'm comfortable and content with the small crew we have. Whereas Cleophus wants to be larger than life."

"Give him a few days. He'll come around," she said before planting a kiss on the back of my hand.

Shaking my head, I replied, "I'm afraid if I don't come around, Cleophus and my friendship will end. Nana, I don't want what he wants. Do you know how much shit can come from it? Orthello, OG Buckingham and Auntie Rebecca's son, will do whatever it takes to see him and a few of his men running the crew. Blood will be shed, and I promise you ... our small crew isn't going to be the ones to die. Nana, I don't want to slaughter my auntie's sons and nephews by marriage because of what my partner wants. I don't want to do that, and it seems that Cleophus see shit one way—his way."

§§§

Dinner with my lady was nice, but I wished there wasn't a dark cloud over my head. Gazing at the beautiful woman wasn't enough to pull me out of my funk. For the first time since NaTashia returned, I had the displeasure of feeling unhappiness and turmoil. I didn't want to feel that way. Rightfully, I expected Cleophus to hold his position as my right hand.

The more I thought about the situation, the more I felt like I had to bow to him. I didn't want to do that to ensure our friendship stayed intact. I did that shit enough when we were younger. I was his ride or die partner, no matter what. Too much was at stake, and honestly, I wasn't up for putting NaTashia and our kids in harm's way. They had never lived like that before, and they sure as hell weren't going to start now.

Mullage's "Trick'n" played at a nice decibel from the TV's speakers in my room. As I laid on the bed, I opened my eyes, smiling at the sight before me. NaTashia sauntered towards me, looking edible than a motherfucker. The red lingerie, two-piece outfit clung to her body perfectly. Her naturally curly and bushy hair was shoved into a messy yet sexy ponytail.

"What you got going on, woman?" I smiled before licking my lips and profoundly inhaling the sweet-scent perfume sauntering from her body.

Sexily climbing over me, she said, "I need to get you out of that funk. I can't have you moping around because of Cleophus ill-thinking behind."

Rubbing her ankles, I asked, "Just how are you going to pull me out of my funk, Nana?"

With a raised eyebrow, she bit her bottom lip, all the while placing the tip of her finger in the corner of her mouth and said, "I think I have a few ways to pull you *all* the way out of your blues, sir."

"Is that so?" I probed, sliding further towards the headboard.

"Yep," she voiced, slowly winding onto my man.

Tony Toni Tone's "Whatever You Want" played and NaTashia said, "Ah, shit now."

As I chuckled, the sexy woman slow danced on me, all the while taking off my shirt. While singing the song to me and capturing my undivided attention, my mind was only on NaTashia and our future together.

With my shirt off, she seductively slid down my body, unbuckling my belt and pants. Eye fucking me, NaTashia took off my pants before throwing them on the floor.

"Whatever you want," she beautifully sang, gazing into my eyes.

My man was bricked. The urge to have NaTashia's legs to the ceiling was at an all-time high. I refrained from doing so because I needed the show she was putting on for me. It was better to have the real deal than to fantasize about it.

The beat dropped to one of her favorite twerking songs. Crunk as ever, NaTashia damn near fell off the bed; I had to catch her ass. While holding onto her ankles, I laughed so damn hard I started coughing.

"That shit isn't funny, Fabian," she stated, giggling.

"Yes, it is," I replied, pulling her towards me.

"On some serious stuff, I just spooked the hell out of myself. I don't even want to dance on the bed anymore," she voiced, sitting in Indian-style, gazing at me.

Still laughing, I replied, "You ain't going to start something and don't finish just because you almost knocked your-damn-self out. Get your head together, and let's continue."

"While I gather myself, how about you dance for me?" she asked, eye sexing me.

"You are pushing it," I chuckled, rubbing her thigh.

Laying her head on my stomach, she said, "No, I'm not. I want to see you slap that dick up and down and twirl it around."

Laughing, I replied, "A'ight. Hold up for a minute."

Shocked, she asked, "You going to do it for real?"

"Yep," I voiced with a smile on my face.

As she moved off me, Ball Greezy's "I Gotta Thang Fa You" played. Exiting the bed, I bobbed my head and moved in sync with the song.

"Get it, get it," I stated, vibing with the music.

Waiting for the right beat to make my dick jump before I twirled, I looked at the ceiling. NaTashia started cheering and chanting. By the fourth shout of her impatient behind, I gave my woman precisely what she asked for.

"Get it, get it! Yasss, throw that dick in that air," she happily squealed, clapping her hands.

Once the song ended, one of our favorite local artist's songs played. That damn NaTashia almost fell again, but that didn't stop her from hopping in my face, rapping, and jigging. Loving our vibing time, I thought it was best to create our own club. Thus, I exited the room with her on my heels, rapping.

"Now, everybody wanna be down wit' the south!" she hollered as I grabbed a bottle of Grey Goose and two shot cups.

As the previous song ended, replaced by Ginuwine's "None of Your Friends Business", I asked, "Do you want a chaser?"

Shaking her head, she said, "Nope."

"A'ight," I voiced, looking at my woman dancing for me.

As I posted up in front of the counter, I imagined fucking her against every wall in the kitchen before taking her to the living room and ravishing her ass.

Seeing her body was lonely without mine close to hers, I sauntered towards her. As we slow danced, NaTashia draped her arms around my shoulder and gazed into my eyes. Those peepers had me shook and falling more in love with her.

They were dreamy and mesmerizing. Those types of eyes were the kind any man would fall weak for. I didn't blame that nigga Joseph for shacking up with NaTashia. Those eyes and her persona were enough to make any man recant being married and having a family.

"Kissin' you, touchin' you," I sang along with Profyle's "Feelin' This" as I rubbed on my baby's backside.

"I'm glad you are calm and enjoying yourself, Fabian," she softly spoke, looking into my eyes.

"Me too. Thank you for pulling me off the cliff," I gently replied, squeezing her rounded bottom.

"Anytime," she stated, biting the corner of her juicy and glossy bottom lip.

"Fuckk," I groaned.

"What?" she asked, massaging the nape of my neck.

"I love the way we are right now. I don't ever want it to end. Promise me, we will never end. We will continue to grow, Nana?"

"I promise we will never end, and we will continue to grow," she sincerely announced before planting a sweet and delicate kiss upon my lips.

"I know I shouldn't be asking you this, but I got to ... did he ever slow dance with you?"

"Yes."

"Was it anything like what we are doing? Well, did you feel the way you feel now with me towards him?"

Shaking her head, she replied, "Not even close."

"How did y'all meet?"

"Two months into me being in Atlanta, I was a teller at a bank. He was a customer. Upon coming to my work station to deposit a check, he wrote his name and number on a piece of paper and passed it to me. New to the area, I needed to get out and have fun. So, that weekend, I called him. We met up, had a nice evening out."

"Ah," I voiced, jealous.

"We continued going on dates and having fun. A month into knowing each other, I lost my virginity to him. Three months later, things took off like a rocket. I was smitten, but I wasn't in love. I was well-cared for, but I still wasn't pleased. I longed for something, someone, but I couldn't quite put my finger on it, or it could've been I didn't want to realize I had made a mistake in leaving Alabama. It wasn't until after I became pregnant with Maxon, I realized something. What I realized caused me to cry many nights. What I had known deep down had me upset at myself, resulting in me staying away for so long. Then, I had Angel. I knew all hope was lost after her, so I put the 'what if's' behind me and dealt with the hand I had given myself."

As Barry White's "I've Got So Much to Give" played, NaTashia continued talking. While she did so, she didn't look into my face. She stared at my chest. At that moment, I knew she was airing out her truths; something she had known for years while she was away with another man; a man who loved her just as much as I did.

With teary eyes, she looked at me and said, "I'm so sorry I didn't come back to *you*, Fabian. I'm sorry I left *us* in the dust. I'm sorry I didn't build a family with *you*. Don't get me wrong, I don't regret being in Joseph's life and vice versa because that's not the case. I hate I didn't give *us* a chance that I'm giving *us* right now."

Massaging the nape of her neck, I replied, "Don't blame yourself, Nana. Honestly, I don't fault you; I fault myself. I could've said something, but I didn't. I was a coward for sending you away with six thousand dollars, a hug, and well wishes."

"That was you who put six thousand dollars into my bag?" she asked, shocked.

"Yeah," I replied nodding.

"Well, shit. I thought it was Cleophus, which I thanked him for."

Laughing, I replied, "I know. He emphasized how much you thanked him for everything he did."

"Well, what did he do?"

"The apartment he found, the first month's rent, and half of the furniture."

"And you paid the deposit and the other half of the furniture."

"Yep."

"Oh, wow. Do you think any of that money he paid was from Willie Buckingham?"

"To think about it, I'm sure Cleophus paid the initial monies from his own pocket and gave you the money OG Buckingham handed him for you. To get a better understanding, you might want to ask your uncle."

"Okay," she voiced, eyeing me.

While we let the soft melodies of Hi-Five take our bodies to a happy place, our eyes never left the other. Close to the end of the song, NaTashia said, "Fabian?"

"Yes?" I responded, looking down at the average height woman, who was shorter than me.

"For what it's worth, Joseph didn't compare to you. Rest assured, I wasn't anywhere near as elated to be with him as I am with you. Whatever you think, never think for a second you are a rebound guy. Never feel as if I would never choose you. If I could do it all over again, I would choose you in a heartbeat. I will always choose you. Just because I had children with him doesn't mean he was superior to you. No man on this earth will ever hold weight in my heart like you do," she genuinely spoke.

Feeling every word that left her mouth, my need for her love intensified. Within a heartbeat, I sucked her lips into my mouth as I lifted her off the ground. Carrying her to the nearest wall, my hands explored as her coos flowed down my throat. Pinning her up against the wall, I snatched off the red thong before dropping it on the floor.

With her legs dangling off my shoulders, I glared into her eyes and loving said, "Thank you for reassuring me why you are my everything, and always will be."

Chapter Eleven

NaTashia

Wednesday, December 11th

As DJ Trans "Ride Out" blasted throughout our home, I danced and performed my daily duties of cleaning the house. The house wasn't dirty, but I believed in cleaning every day and dusting often. Maxon had issues with dust allergies. If my poor boy received a whiff of dust, he would be sneezing until his nose started to hurt.

Ring. Ring. Ring.

Muting the TV, I grabbed my cell phone out of my pocket and glanced at the screen. Instantly, a huge smile was on my face.

Answering the phone, I sang, "Hello."

"How is my favorite and most loved woman doing?" Fabian asked.

"Missing the shit out of you, but I'm good. How are you? How's California?"

"I'm about to go insane from missing you, and I'm about to lose my shits dealing with your egotistical uncle. California is cool. It would be a lot better if you and the kids were here with me," he replied as Cleophus hollered for Fabian to stop whining like a little broad.

"Go fuck yourself, nigga!" Fabian spat, heated.

As Cleophus clapped back, Fabian sighed heavily and asked, "Did Angel give you any trouble getting up this morning?"

"Thankfully, no," I rapidly replied before asking, "I see y'all little trip is making things worse, huh?"

"More than you would ever know. I'm fifteen seconds away from renting a car and bringing my ass home. I told you I didn't want to take this trip in the first place. It's a waste of time, Nana."

"Yet, you took your ass along because you don't trust anyone else to be with Cleophus."

"And I'm about ready to say fuck this shit," he spoke in an agitated tone as Cleophus's loud voice boomed in the background.

"You have one more day, baby. Deal with it. Okay?"

"I'll try," he quickly voiced before asking, "On another note, what you did so far today?"

"Cleaned the house and prepared dinner. Oh, yeah, I rearranged the bedrooms."

Laughing, he said, "Shit, you are bored."

"Especially since you are gone. Um, what do you think about me getting a part-time gig?"

"I don't like it, but if that's what you want to do ... then, I will support you. Where are you looking at?"

"Actually, nowhere. I'm looking at being self-employed."

"In the fashion department?"

"Yes."

"In that case, I do like it. Shoot for it. What do you need?"

"A better sewing machine, someone to draw, my own space, and other accessories."

"As far as your own space, you can have my man-cave for the time being. I'll talk to a contractor about adding another room to the house for your workspace. Order everything you need. Use the black card in your wallet."

"You do know I have my own money, right?" I stated sassily with my hands on my hips and a smirk upon my face.

"And you do know I have money to spend on anything you need and want, right?" Fabian provocatively and savagely spoke.

Turned on, I replied, "In that case, I'll use the black card. Does that please milord?"

In a fake British accent, Fabian responded, "Yes, it does, milady."

While we talked, I felt as if I was a young one again. I giggled, blushed, and pranced about twirling my hair. The way Fabian made me feel was indescribable. I never had a man who made butterflies float around my body as he did. The smile on my face was more expansive than The Joker's. With Fabian, I was okay with life. Thanks to him, I knew I was on the right path of having utter peace, joy, and love—like I had always wanted.

Ding. Dong.

"Who is it?" I loudly asked, looking at the door.

"Liddia Minnow," the woman stated, causing me to gasp.

"Who's at the door, NaTashia? You gasped," Fabian inquired curiously.

"My children's father, wife or widower, whichever you prefer," I stated, slowly walking towards the door.

"How does she know where you are?"

"That's a damn good question," I voiced as I arrived at the door, looking through the peephole. Beside the well-dressed woman were two children.

As I pondered why they were at the doorstep of my home, Fabian asked, "Are you going to let her in?"

"Should I?" I lowly asked.

"Yes. Put the past behind you so you and *our* kids can move on. We are yet to tell them about us."

"Okay," I voiced, opening the door.

While unlocking the screen door, I told Fabian I would call him back. As I invited Liddia and her kids into the cozy house, she politely asked, "Hi. Um, is there somewhere private we can talk?"

"The kitchen," I stated, pointing in that direction.

"Are your children home?"

"No, they are in school," I replied, locking the screen door.

Liddia informed her children she was going to talk with me for a bit. The well-mannered children sat on the sofa, lost and confused.

Before exiting the living room, I placed the TV on a cartoon channel.

As we walked into the kitchen, my curious mind got the best of me. I didn't give Liddia time to tell me why she was in my face or how she knew where I lived. I fired the questions off as I pulled out a chair. After she told me how she found me, via Ethan and then my mother, Liddia hopped straight into why she was sitting in my face.

"I had some time to think about the way I handled things after Joseph's death. Also, I had time to reflect on the letter he left me. He explained that he didn't inform you of our marriage since I was giving him a hard time about the divorce. Even in death, he spoke extremely stern yet loving and thoughtful words towards you and your children. Joseph was right; our kids must know each other and build a bond. I knew and love my siblings, and they should love each other, as well. I came here to ask you can we be adults and allow our children to true siblings?"

With a light and warm heart, I nodded and replied, "I would love that. Does Joseph's family feel the same way as you do?"

Shaking her head, she replied, "Unfortunately, they don't. They are old school, stuck-up people, honestly."

"I see," I voiced, not liking her statement.

For the next hour, Liddia and I became more acquainted with each other. The first time we met, I swore she was an uptight, heartless bitch; in fact, she was the complete opposite. She was in love with a man who didn't love her the same way. Their marriage wasn't arranged, but their union was best for their families. Being in a loveless marriage, I couldn't take it. I would've been given him the walking papers. Going before God to start a blissful union for the sake of my family, I wouldn't dare.

Upon our time coming to a closure, I told Liddia what time my kids would arrive home from school. She promised she would return forty minutes after they were settled in. While walking her to the door, Rebecca stepped on the porch.

What in the hell does she want? I thought as I sent Liddia and her children away with pleasantries.

"Hey, darling," Rebecca stated as she slipped into the house, standing tall and strong.

"Hi," I spoke politely.

"Um, I came by to tell you of your father's funeral plan in case you wanted to come," she softly spoke.

"Thank you, but I won't be attending."

"It would be a good way to get to know the family," she insisted.

Becoming frustrated with the woman, I sighed deeply but respectfully and said, "It may be, but I don't want those troubles. Like I said before, I didn't know him. There's no need for little ole me to stir up trouble when I'm not trying to do that. I want to live in peace and harmony. I don't like drama, or do I participate in drama-filled activities. I'm sure you can understand my position on the matter."

"I do. Believe me, I do," she stated, taking a seat on the sofa.

While looking at me, Rebecca patted the cushion next to her. I didn't want to communicate with the woman, yet I sucked it up. After all, she was Fabian's auntie.

"You know, NaTashia, love and family are the two most important things in life. To me, they are more important than money and materialistic things. Out of all the materialistic stuff I own, I rather have family and love," she stated gently, grabbing my hand.

As the woman carried on, I actively listened. I knew where the story was headed, and I had a rebuttal for her ass.

"I don't want us to be strangers because of the situation, NaTashia. I made a mistake many years ago with my sister, Fabian's mother. I chose the materialistic shit over my sister and nephew. To this day, I regret allowing my sister to turn her back on me. I regret not being in my nephew's life, as I should've been. Now, I'm trying to make up for lost time. I said all of that to say this, allow people into your life that will give you the happiest moments and the prized possession of being loved and cared for. Don't alienate yourself because you fear drama. Let people in; let them see what's unique inside of your heart and soul. Only a miserable and bitter person wouldn't give you the love you much deserve. I have talked to my children and expressed how I felt about the matter. Of course, with expressing how I felt … I had to tell them why I felt this way. They are willing to sit down and talk to you. Most importantly, I want everyone to be cordial because there will be a day, my nephew asks you to marry him. I have a feeling you will hesitate to say yes because of this triangle. I *need* us to be on a better front so his heart won't break again.

I *need* you to allow my children and me into your heart so you and Fabian can have the life y'all deserve together," she spoke wholeheartedly with tears in her eyes.

As I glared at the beautifully aged woman, I nodded and said, "Okay."

Kissing the back of my hand several times, she responded, "Thank you. Thank you so much."

There was a long moment of silence between us before she said, "I've taken up enough of your time. If you decide to come to the funeral, it'll be this Saturday at 1 p.m. at First Episcopal Missionary Church."

"All right. If I'm not comfortable coming to the church, I will be present at the repast, if that's okay."

Standing and smiling, she voiced, "That's more than okay."

While walking her to the door, I felt an overwhelming sensation cruise through my body. I wasn't sure why it felt so strong upon her saying, "Step out on faith. Treasure each day with those you love as if it's your last day. Love as hard and as much as you can. Never be afraid to tell someone just how much you love and can't live without them, NaTashia. Never let anyone leave your life that only wants the best for you. Do you understand what I'm saying?"

Nodding, I honestly replied, "I do."

After we embraced in a loving hug, I closed and locked the door, all the while grabbing my phone. The message Rebecca had given me was loud and clear; it wasn't what I initially thought. As I dialed Fabian's number, my hand shook.

"Hello," he handsomely said as I heard Plies "Ran Off On Da Plug Twice" play.

"Yes, I'll marry you," I happily voiced as tears slid down my face.

The volume on the radio was turned down as he excitedly said, "Come again?"

Loudly, I announced, "Your black ass heard me the first time ... yes, I'll marry you!"

Instantly, he started hooting and hollering. As I laughed, Cleophus shouted, "Bitch, you scared me! What the fuck is wrong with you, nigga? We traveling with all this damn dope! I'm swerving and shit! Chill, nigga!"

"Man, fuck you!" Fabian laughed before continuing, "My woman said she'll marry me, niggaaaaa!"

"'Bout fuckin' time!" Cleophus and June Bug replied before hooting and hollering along with Fabian.

While they carried on, I plopped on the lounge chair. Shortly afterward, Fabian asked, "When do you want to become my wife, Nana?"

"Soon."

"Start planning it. We are heading back to 'Bama now," he happily stated.

Excited but curious, I asked, "I thought y'all had one more day. What caused y'all to leave out early?"

"The shopping took place earlier than we had decided," he replied.

In other words, their supplier gave them the drugs earlier.

Smiling, I said, "Gotcha. Y'all be safe, and I love you so much, Fabian."

"You know my love for you is like none other. You have no idea how happy you made me, Nana. As always, I will be safe."

After blowing kisses into the phone, we ended the call. Overly emotional, I stood, tears streaming down my face and butterflies flip-flopping in my stomach.

Excitedly, I hollered, "I'm going to marry my best friend! I'm going to marry that black ass nigga!"

Chapter Twelve

Fabian

Friday, December 13th

At eight o'clock a.m., I dropped down in the city. I was eager to get to my lady. Thanks to Cleophus and June Bug's asses, we didn't arrive home as soon as I thought we would. Those fools wanted to stop at several hot cities in Texas and Louisiana. Of course, those assholes partied and shopped as if we didn't have numerous bricks in the trunk of the car. My antsy behind wasn't up for partying or doing anything out of the ordinary. Yet, I was outnumbered, so I had to suck it up.

Ring. Ring. Ring.

"Damn, is we at home yet?" June Bug inquired sleepily from the back seat.

"Yeah."

"About time. I'm tired of being in this car," he fussed.

"We would've been home if y'all asses didn't want to stop in all those fucking cities," I voiced at him while pressing the answer option.

"Hey. Where are y'all?" NaTashia asked worriedly.

"We in the city. I'm bypassing South Court Street exit now."

"Really?" she voiced excitedly.

"Really," I replied, smiling.

"Well, in that case, I need you to get off the next exit and circle back towards the county courthouse."

With a raised eyebrow, I hopped in the far right lane and asked, "A'ight, but um, for what though?"

"So, we can turn in our marriage license."

"Shid, you ain't got to say that shit twice, Nana. I'm on my way now," I voiced, mashing on the gas pedal.

"Bitch, you lost yo' mind. We got bricks upon bricks in this bitch," June Bug and Cleophus spat, looking at me as if I was crazy.

"Fuck y'all and these bricks, bitches." I laughed.

"I swear y'all talk to each other as if y'all are females," NaTashia laughed.

"What you thought that would change upon us getting older?" I inquired chuckling.

"Um, yeah."

"Hell no. Sorry to disappoint you," I chuckled as I aimed towards the county courthouse.

"Why we ain't going to the crib, dude?" Cleophus asked, agitated.

"Bitch, I'm finna turn in my marriage license. You finna drive back to the house," I told him as I playfully shoved his head.

"Oooh, you black bitch, you better be glad you are my day one. I swear I would pop yo' ass upside the head like Mrs. Lola used to do," Cleophus spat, causing NaTashia, June Bug, and I to laugh.

"So, y'all made up?" NaTashia questioned.

"Yes."

"He saw your point of view?"

"More like he saw June Bug's and my point of view."

"Good. Good. I swore I didn't want to beat my uncle across the back for getting you in a mood I didn't like."

Smiling, I said, "My ride or die."

"Always."

Knowing I needed to holler at my partners, I said, "Aye, baby, I'll be there in a minute."

"Okay. I'm sitting in Bessie. As always, you can't help but see her."

"A'ight. I love you."

"I love you more."

Ending the call, I briefly glanced at Cleophus before looking in the rearview mirror at a closed-eye June Bug.

"Y'all know I love y'all to the moon and back, right?"

"Nigga, don't start that mushy shit, nih!" June Bug yelled, resulting in Cleophus laughing.

"I'm serious, dude. I wouldn't have gotten this far without y'all as y'all wouldn't have gotten this far without me. I want to be one hundred about everything. If Nana asks me to leave this shit alone, y'all know I'm gone, right?"

In unison, they replied, "Yep."

"Would y'all be on some salty shit if that happens?"

"If it was another broad, hell yeah, but that's fam. She and the kids will always come first," Cleophus voiced sincerely as June Bug agreed.

"But, bitch, when we say brang them toys out because we in som' shit, nigga you better brang yo' ass out that doe wit' all those fancy-ass sniper guns you got," June Bug seriously voiced.

Nodding, I replied, "No doubt. No doubt."

As I neared my destination, Cleophus sat upright and said, "You spend the day wit' my niece. I'm sure y'all have a lot of shit to handle. If y'all need someone to get them after school, I'll have Santana to pick up Maxon and Angel."

"I highly doubt we will need y'all today, but I will keep that in mind."

"That lil' one, Maxon, be in heaven when Santana is 'round," June Bug chuckled.

"Hell yeah, he do. He be at my woman hard. He kills me, acting like he's an infant. Lil' nigga don' asked my woman to tuck him into bed, and she happily tucks him in." Cleophus laughed, shaking his head.

"Bruhhh," June Bug and I spoke in unison, chuckling.

Letting the jokes go, I became serious as I sighed deeply. Cleophus had a ride or die chick by his side; yet, he was too stubborn to see it, or it could've been he was scared to fully open up to her. Either way, he had to let go and give Santana his all as she's been giving him her all.

"Aye, Cleophus, on a serious tip, you need to settle down with Santana. She's been down with you for a hot minute. She's a good fit for you," I told Cleophus, eyeing him closely.

"I know. Ever since Nana told you she would marry you, I've been thinkin' 'bout poppin' the question to her. I was going to tag along wit' you when you copped my niece a ring."

"I had been copped a ring for Nana many years ago. Since she been back, I've had it on me," I replied, pulling beside Bessie.

"What?" they hollered in unison. June Bug sat upright and stared at me.

"An' you didn't say shit 'bout it?" Cleophus stated, punching me in the arm.

As I opened the door, I replied, "Nope. Now, I will be over June Bug's crib when we finish handling this."

"Nawl, nigga, you go be wit' yo' fiancée. I been waitin' a long time to see y'all together like this. Cleophus an' I got this. Take two days off wit' Nana an' the kids," June Bug stated as he and Cleophus opened the doors.

"Bet," I replied as we dapped.

Stepping out of the car, looking fabulous, NaTashia sweetly and happily voiced, "There he goes. I have been missing him something awful."

With a smile on my face as I strolled towards her, I replied, "I've been missing you equally something awful."

As I snatched NaTashia off her feet and spun her around, my mouth found its way to her neck. While I planted many kisses on her neck, June Bug and Cleophus greeted my woman from the car.

"Well, hello, there, fellas." She smiled, waving as I placed her on the ground.

"You finally finna lock his ass down, huh?" June Bug asked.

"Yes," she smiled.

"Good. Tired of seein' that nigga walkin' 'round like a sick dog," Cleophus voiced, hopping out of the back seat.

"Ah, bitch nigga, be quiet." I laughed as I dropped to one knee.

Those foolish idiots started hooting and hollering, all the while clapping.

My beautiful woman smiled, cheeks darkening and eyes lightening up like our Christmas tree once the kids turned it on.

"We are doing this backward, but I don't give a damn. You said yes, and that's good enough for me, Nana, but um..." I stated as I reached into my front pocket for her engagement ring.

"Oou, bitch, I just know you ain't had that damn ring on you all this time and didn't attempt to let us see it!" Cleophus hollered like a broad.

Turning to face him, I said, "You was acting like a little broad the entire trip, and it ceased my mind to show it to y'all."

"My apologies," he voiced.

"All is forgiven," I quickly told him as I placed my eyes back on my woman.

Glaring into NaTashia's mesmerizing eyes, I sincerely spoke, "Since the first day I placed my hands on your back and shoved you off the swinger, I knew you would be in my life forever. There has never been a second I didn't want you around me, gazing into my eyes. I love everything about you to the point it drives me insane. I want nothing more than to wake up to you every morning and go to bed with you every night. All I've ever wanted to do was create a beautiful life with you. On this lovely muggy day, I'm the luckiest and happiest man to walk into that courthouse and sign my name on the dotted line to be your loving, kind, and protective man. I vow to love Maxon and Angel as my own as I have been doing. NaTashia, thank you so much for giving me the best holiday gift I've had in a long time. Thank you for giving me my life back with two precious beings to spoil every day of our lives. You've said you would marry me, but let me do it the right way. Will you marry me, NaTashia Robertson?"

Wiggling her left ring finger, she happily voiced, "Yes, yes, and yes, Fabian Wells."

As I slipped the ring onto her finger, June Bug and Cleophus clapped and congratulated us. While kissing my lovely woman, the fellas told us they would talk to us later. I chunked the deuces at my pals before they pulled off.

Patting my chest, NaTashia pulled away and asked, "Shall we?"

Grabbing her hand, I replied, "We shall."

While crossing the street, NaTashia told me of wedding dates she was thinking of. I didn't like any of the dates. I preferred Christmas Eve during the night hours.

"Why?" she inquired as we climbed the few steps.

Smiling, I said, "Everybody opens one gift on Christmas Eve. I want our union to be my gift. We step into a new life together, happily married."

"Well, Christmas Eve it will be. Do you have an exact time?" she inquired as Orthello stepped out of the courthouse.

"Nine o'clock p.m. I want our wedding to start. We will bring Christmas in with our close loved ones and friends," I told her as I didn't take my eyes off my mean-mugging cousin.

I felt as if he had something he wanted to get off his chest. Thus, I kissed NaTashia before telling her, "You head to our destination ... I will be there shortly."

Seeing there was tension close by, she hesitated for a second before giving in to what I needed her to do. I waited until she was out of earshot before I addressed the elephant glaring into my face.

Strolling towards my cousin with my head held high and shoulders upright, I asked, "You need to get something off your chest, Orthello?"

"Yep, but this isn't the place or time to do so," the tall, lean, and deep-voiced individual spat.

Chuckling, I stepped in his space and glared into his long shaped face. Tired of staring at the nigga, I spoke my mind. "You are upset because of your father's and OG Mag's decision of Cleophus and I running their organization.

Trust, we don't want that dump. We are not taking the offer. There isn't enough stupidity in us to accept the offer. The way y'all moving … none of you niggas will be on the streets longer than three years. Half of those niggas won't live long enough to see two Christmases. Y'all niggas think you know everything but don't know shit. You won't sit long enough or shut the fuck up for a split second to learn something. So, believe me when I say we don't want the hassle of training grown men how to trap … we don't. So, feel free to step to OG Mag. He'll gladly give you what Cleophus and I won't accept. Now, if you don't mind … I have a beautiful woman waiting for me to sign my name on the dotted line, right beside hers. Peace and blessings to you and your new crew, cousin. By the way, I will be present to show respect to your dad, and I *expect* no shit to pop off."

As I stepped away from Orthello, the expression on his face was priceless. The nigga didn't have anything to say; thus, he dropped his head and sighed heavily. My cousin had to have known I was right about everything I spoke on. Hell, it was a blessing he was still alive and free of a prison cell.

Stepping into the cool lobby of the county courthouse, NaTashia worriedly gazed at me and asked, "Is everything okay?"

Nodding my head as I pulled her close to me, I responded, "Yep, and it always will be. Are you ready to take the first step of being my wife?"

"Actually, sir, this is the second step to being your wife," she stated lovingly, pulling me towards the metal detectors.

§§§

"Soooo, Fabian and I have something to tell y'all," NaTashia voiced as Angel was curled underneath her mother, and Maxon was to the right of me.

"What y'all have to tell us?" Maxon asked, looking into my face.

"Remember when I told y'all Fabian and I are best friends?" NaTashia voiced, looking between the quiet children.

"Yes," they replied in unison.

"Well, it's a great thing that we are best friends and always will be. Our love for one another is amazing and beautiful. So, beautiful, we have decided to get married. What do y'all think about that?"

"I like it," Angel exclaimed with a smile on her face.

Maxon didn't say anything; therefore, I rubbed the top of his head and asked, "What about you?"

"I'm confused," he quickly spoke, bringing a smile to my face.

"What are you confused about, buddy?"

"Like how can you be our godfather and marry our mom? Why would best friends marry each other? You supposed to be friends, right?"

"In the beginning, when your mom and I put an entire list together for best friend rules, we agreed we would care for each other's children for the rest of our lives. The older we became, the more I fell in love with your mother. Keep in mind, she was still my friend. I didn't treat her any differently. I still saw the amazing, loving, smart, and kind woman as my friend. In my opinion, especially when it concerns marriage, your partner should be your best friend. You should be able to tell them anything. They should be the first one you want to tell everything to. Even though we are getting married … your mother will always be my friend. She's the only person I want to tell everything to."

By the expression on his face, Maxon was still lost. I looked at NaTashia, smiling.

"Maxon, honey," she softly asked before continuing, "How do you feel about the matter?"

"I'm lost on the friendship and marriage thing, but I'm okay with y'all getting married," he replied rapidly, clearly shoving the conversation to the side.

"You know you can tell or ask us anything, right?" I told him.

Nodding, he responded, "Yes."

For the thirty minutes, NaTashia and I tried talking to Maxon. He dryly responded, and his answers were straight to the point. It was apparent he didn't want to talk about us getting married. The entire time I observed Maxon, I was sure he was conflicted about our marriage. There was no doubt in my mind he was thinking about his dad and mom. He was used to his dad being around and in their lives on a loving note. I was sure he thought one day they would be married.

"Hey, Maxon," I voiced, requesting his undivided attention.

"Sir?" he lowly voiced, eyes showed he was sad.

"No matter what, I will never replace your dad. He will always hold that title. I will never shove him out of the way. Okay?" I genuinely stated, glaring into his eyes.

With a smile on his face, he said, "Okay. So, I won't have to call you, dad, right? Because I love my dad even though he's dead."

Nodding, I replied, "Unless you want to, but I won't put any pressure on you or your sister. I know you love him, and you should even though he's not here with you in the flesh."

We had finally broken the ice with little man, and all was well. The walls within the house resumed to joyful noise and chaos. Our family night was perfect. We did everything together, cooked, cleaned, and settled on the sofa with snacks as our eyes were on the TV. Throughout the family movie, I was beyond emotional. I had the perfect life with the most amazing people in it. My heart was content as my soul was overjoyed and at peace. I couldn't have asked for more than I already had. In my mind, I was the wealthiest person alive. I had what many wished they could have—true love and an unlimited supply of happiness.

Around ten-thirty or so, I placed the sleeping children in their beds. Before I exited their rooms, I planted a kiss on their foreheads and whispered for them to sleep tight.

Walking into the living room, NaTashia had turned off the TV and majority of the lights except for one, the stove light. From my man cave, slow jams played at a nice listening volume. A smile spread across my face as I sauntered towards the chilling and thinking room. Upon entering the candlelit area, I witnessed the romantic job NaTashia had done. There were several covers on the floor and two pillows a few inches away from the covers' top edge. Fake, red rose petals were placed on the blankets and pillows.

"Do you like it?" she asked, lighting the last candle as I closed and locked the door.

"Most definitely," I stated, strolling towards her.

"So, I think our conversation went well with the kids," she said, placing the candle on the entertainment center.

"As do I," I replied, in arms reach of the sexy being.

Resting her head on my chest, we fell in sync with Al Green's "Let's Stay Together". Of course, I had to do the most and sing along. I couldn't sing to save my life, but I didn't give a damn. NaTashia laughed as she poorly egged me on.

"Oou, loving your forever, is what I need," I sang horribly, grabbing her hand and dancing.

As I pulled her close to me, we sang together, "Ooh, baby, let's ... let's stay together."

Upon the end of the song, our lips locked as if they were love bugs. As our tongues danced, so did our hands. Cuffing her rounded bottom, I lifted NaTashia in the air. Quickly and smoothly, she wrapped her legs around my waist.

While I descended towards the covers, NaTashia asked with a wicked smile upon her face, "You don't have any plans for tomorrow morning, do you?

"None at all," I replied, laying her on the covers.

"Are you sure?" she said, ensuring to show me the tip of her tongue.

A chill ran through my body as I nodded and voiced, "Absolutely sure. The fellas ordered me to be away for the next two days."

"Is that so?" she seductively stated, pushing me onto my back.

"Yep," I groaned.

"Good. I think you will be sleeping in tomorrow morning," she stated, eyeing me and removing my dick out of my boxers.

"Shid, I'm with it," I slurred.

"Ready for a couple rounds of nightcaps?" she asked before licking the head of my man.

"I'm beyond ready," I groaned, eyes fluttering.

"Good because I'm ready to saddle up and have a few long and rough, and then smooth yet exciting rides," she provocatively spoke, eyeing me and talking into my dick as if it was a microphone.

Chapter Thirteen

NaTashia

Thursday, December 19th

When I opened my crusty eyes this morning, I realized I hadn't shopped for Christmas, which was six days away. After planting several kisses on Fabian's forehead and mouth, I hopped to my feet with my cell phone in my hand. I didn't want to go shopping by myself. I was tired of doing that; so, I called Cleophus. I was sure Santana wasn't far from my uncle. After chatting with her for a brief second, we agreed I would pick her up within thirty minutes for a day of shopping and bonding.

The moment the bubbly and beautiful chick hopped in the car, we chatted as if we were best friends. Without a doubt, I understood why my uncle wouldn't let her go. She was a gem. In many ways, she reminded me of myself. Without a doubt, I knew we would become great friends.

After becoming more acquainted with one another, we packed our shopping carts and talked about my wedding. The more questions Santana asked, the more I realized Fabian and I hadn't done any planning. We barely talked about our wedding night. Immediately, I knew I had to get the ball rolling. Our time was slowly running out.

While having lunch, Santana took the wheels and led me in the right direction concerning my union with Fabian. In a matter of seconds, she had Cleophus and Fabian on the phone. Fabian hopped off the phone first to contact Aunt Marilyn to see if she could watch Maxon and Angel. Cleophus stated he was on his way over to Fabian's to pick him up. Within an hour, the guys were in our presence, being their usual goofy selves.

We visited every bridal store in the city, and I wasn't impressed. Fabian suggested we go to bridal stores in Birmingham. Before we left the city, Fabian decided he wanted Bessie to get out of the town for the day. Like happy schoolgirls, Santana and I chanted, ranted, and raved. My uncle wasn't far behind us with his bullshit. After dropping Cleophus's car off at our home, we hit the road with me in the driver's seat.

Along the way talks of Willie Buckingham's funeral and repast came about. With so much happiness going on around me, I forgot about his funeral and the promise I made to Rebecca. I wanted to deaden the entire conversation; however, Cleophus and Fabian wouldn't shut up until I told them I wasn't going to the funeral, but I would be present for the repast. Satisfied with my answer, the topic was changed to a more interesting one.

When we arrived at the galleria and stepped across the mall's door's threshold, many memories flooded my mind. It was a large group of us skipping school during our second semester of tenth grade. Fabian's and Cleophus's groupies were pissed because of the numerous amounts of bags I held.

"Thinkin' 'bout the old days, huh?" Cleophus asked, looking at me.

"Yes."

"Those were the days," Fabian voiced.

"Yes, it was," I stated.

Simultaneously, a female loudly called my uncle's and Fabian's names, all the while waving. The female wasn't overly aggressive or anything of that nature. By the way the woman stared at my uncle, and he ceased walking, I knew some shit was about to pop off.

"Cleophus, who is she?" Santana voiced calmly.

"Um ... um ...," he stated as the pretty female approached us, titties bouncing with every step she took.

Through clenched teeth, Santana said, "Cleophus, you better speak before she does."

Like the fool he really was, my uncle didn't say a word. I looked at Santana, and the expression on her face was one I wished I didn't have to witness. I deeply regretted the way she felt. I was sure she feared the worst from the female. Hell, I would've.

"Hey," the woman politely spoke to my uncle.

"What's up?" Cleophus voiced, trying to avoid looking at the woman.

"How have you been?"

"Good."

An awkward silence overcame them as Santana cleared her throat and asked, "If you don't mind me asking, who are you?"

"I'm Bailey. The mother of Cleophus' three kids," she voiced, glaring into Santana's eyes.

I was beyond stunned with an open mouth as Fabian sighed profoundly and sighed, "Oh shit."

My friend's legs buckled as she poorly said, "Three children?"

"Yes," Bailey responded politely.

Placing her eyes on my uncle, Santana asked, "How old are your children, Cleophus?"

While clearing his throat, he didn't look into her eyes. "Three, two, and a few months old."

Loudly, Santana said, "Oh God. Are you serious, Cleophus? Like, please tell me you are joking."

Finally, he placed his eyes on her and said, "No, I'm not joking."

"Wow," she stated before looking at me and saying as calmly as she could, "We are here for you and Fabian. What do you say about finding the perfect items for y'all's special day?"

Knowing she needed to get away from Cleophus, I said, "We can do this another day, Santana."

Rapidly shaking her head, she said, "No, we are going to do this today. I need to do this with you. After your wedding, I'm going back home. There is nothing in the city that's keeping me anymore. So, shall we enjoy this day as if my life hadn't done a three-sixty turn?"

Nodding, I replied, "Okay."

As we walked off, Cleophus called Santana's name. She didn't flinch at the urgency and hurt in his tone. Like the true woman I had believed her to be, Santana held her head high and placed the biggest smile on her face as she aided me in shopping for my special day.

Throughout our time in Birmingham, bouncing from store to store, Santana stayed away from my uncle. At the same time, I wondered did Fabian know about my little cousins; then, I arrived at a conclusion he didn't because he would've told me. Cleophus tried his best to talk to her, but she had an ignore game out of this world. I thought she would've snapped on him for explaining what happened between him and Bailey, but she didn't.

After I tried on three wedding dresses, I slipped towards the men's section, where the fellas were. In a low tone, I asked Fabian in front of my uncle, "Did you know about the kids?"

"Yeah. I'm their godfather."

"And you didn't tell me about them?" I questioned calmly.

"I kept his secret as he asked me to," Fabian casually spoke, glaring into my eyes.

Respecting his answer, I nodded and said, "Okay."

Grabbing my wrist, Fabian asked, "Are you mad at me?"

"No."

Rubbing my cheeks, he probed, "You promise?"

"I promise," I stated, planting a kiss on his lips.

Sitting in front of the mirror, Cleophus said, "I fucked up big time. Niece, how am I supposed to make things right with Santana? I was going to propose to her today."

Shocked, I shook my head and said, "I don't think you can make this one up. Y'all have been dating close to four years, right?"

Nodding, he said, "Yes."

"You have been dealing with another woman the entire time you were dealing with Santana. You had not one child but three with Bailey. Do you really think you deserve to have her? What's unbelievable to me is the fact Santana didn't go bat shit crazy on you. I don't understand how you say you was going to propose but haven't told her about your kids. Another thing, I can't understand how a woman who loves you with everything in her ... didn't and doesn't have any intentions of acting up from what she's learned. You should be worried about why she's not physically showing you she's hurt, especially in your line of business."

From behind me, Santana calmly said, "Because he's not worthy of seeing me act out of character. He did what he does best; hurt people more than he could ever know. As far as his line of business, I'm not the type of female to bring unnecessary pressure his way; he does have three kids to take care of. The best pressure to apply is to allow him to see me happy with another man who's okay with me not being able to have kids."

Stunned, I turned to face Santana. There were many things I could say, but I didn't.

"I guess that's why he had three children with her. I can't produce. He knew that because we found out together. I gave him the option of leaving me, but he stayed. I had given him a year to leave me, and he didn't. I had an inkling of a feeling that he would have children on me, even though he swore he would never do that. Realistically, what man wouldn't want to have kids? Who would give up the most precious thing in the world, having a family?" she rattled, looking amongst Fabian and me.

"She meant nothing to me, Santana," Cleophus voiced sadly.

Ignoring my uncle's statement, Santana looked at me and asked, "So, did you find your dream dress?"

Nodding, I replied, "I did."

Grabbing my wrist, she weakly smiled and responded, "Well, girlie, it's time to leave Fabian alone so he can find his tuxedo and shoes. I think we have accessories and shoes to shop for, along with discussing the rest of your wedding details."

Standing, Cleophus loudly said, "I need you, Santana. Just hear me out, please. I messed up. I should've told you about my kids. I'm sorry I didn't, but I can't live without you. I refuse to do so. I've never been without you, and I'm not going to start now."

Turning around, she calmly asked, "Oh, you've been without me. You have three children to prove that. So, I'm sure you will be just fine, Cleophus. Make this your last time talking to me, or I just might show you what you've been seeking since I learned your secret. I'm very sure you don't want to see that side of me because you might not make it to see your niece and best friend tie the knot."

§§§

Night had fallen, and I was exhausted. After dealing with a begging Cleophus and a nonchalant Santana, on top of clothes shopping for my wedding and Christmas, I was thankful the kids wanted to stay the night with Auntie Marilyn. Posted up on the headboard, throwing a handful of popcorn in my mouth, I reflected on past and current situations. Instantly, I was thankful for everything I had experienced. I thanked God that I had never been mistreated or used by a man. I thanked the Man above for giving me a sound mind and body.

Laying his head in my lap, Fabian asked, "I love you, NaTashia."

Planting my hand on his chest, I replied, "I love you, sir."

"You've been in a quiet state ever since we dropped Santana off at that hotel. Tell me what's on your mind?" he voiced as my cell phone rang.

"How things played out for them today. It was so sad seeing Santana like that," I said as I saw Cleophus's name on the phone's screen.

"I'm not going to lie; it was rough seeing Santana find out about my godkids like that. I tried telling him he had to come clean to Santana if he wanted to marry her. What I preached, he wasn't listening."

As my phone continued to ring, I silenced it, all the while asking, "Did you know Santana couldn't have kids?"

"Yeah, he told me the day they found out. He was devastated. That was the first time in a while I had seen him cry."

"This Bailey chick, how well do you know her? She did happily greet you as well," I asked, probing.

"When Cleophus didn't want to be bothered with her, I was the one dropping off clothes and money for the kids. I was the middle man in that situation. After the last baby-a boy-was born, Cleophus decided he wanted me to be the godfather of his kids."

"Were y'all there for the birth of his children?"

"Yes, we were. I watched the joyful fool sign their birth certificates. They have his last name. Would you like to see a picture of them?"

"I would love to," I sincerely voiced as Fabian grabbed his cell phone.

Ring. Ring. Ring.

Placing my eyes on the phone, I sighed deeply.

"Please answer your uncle's call before he burns up our text message thread," Fabian spoke, looking at me.

Nodding, I did as my fiancé politely told me.

"Hello," I stated, waiting on Fabian to show me the pictures of my little cousins.

"Aye, Niece, please tell me what hotel Santana's in?" Cleophus voiced painfully.

"I can't do that. I promised I wouldn't tell you."

Breaking down, Cleophus lost it. "I fuckin' need her, NaTashia, just like Fabian needs you to breath. I need her just like that. I made a mistake. I can't do this without her. I was dead ass serious when I said I couldn't live without her. She's my air! Bailey meant nothin' to me. Yes, she has my kids, but my heart doesn't an' never have lied wit' her."

As my uncle sobbed and rambled about his love for Santana, I felt sorry for him. Santana was the only female he had ever cried to me about. I had never witnessed my uncle act the way he did, and honestly, I couldn't help him even if I wanted to. He made his bed; he had to lie in it. I didn't condone a man moving foully towards a woman who gave him the chance to leave her.

"Cleophus," I softly called.

"Huh?" he cried.

Sighing sharply, I said, "I don't know how to help you. I really don't. The best thing I can tell you to do is try calling and texting her. There isn't anything in this world I can say to persuade Santana to stay here. You, of all people, know what it means to get away from the one who hurts you the most. You witnessed it firsthand with me. Simply, Cleophus you fucked up."

"She's changed her number," he replied, sniffling.

"Oh wow," I voiced as my phone dinged in my ear.

Removing the phone, I saw a text message notification from an unknown number. Quickly, I opened the text. It was from Santana. Her message was clear cut—under no circumstances was I to give her new number to Cleophus. Upon replying that I wouldn't, I peacefully and politely ended the call with my foolish uncle.

"You good?" Fabian inquired.

"Yes. Now, may I see my little cousins?" I asked, placing my phone on the nightstand.

As Fabian showed me the beautiful children, two girls and a boy, I ogled the kids. Equally, each of the kids looked like their parents, but they had Cleophus skin hue.

"They are beautiful," I cooed.

"Yes, they are. The oldest one is Layla. The second one Kaliah, and the last one is a junior. Bailey didn't want to name him Cleophus, but of course, your uncle was hell-bent on having his son named after him," Fabian stated as his phone dinged.

There was a brief silence as he read a text message. Sitting upright, my fiancé sighed heavily before saying, "Looks like you will be getting to know them first hand for a few days."

"Why? What's going on?"

"According to Cleophus, Bailey is pissed about what happened today. She's threatening to change their last names and strip away his rights. Trying to do the right thing, Cleophus is heading to Birmingham to get his kids for a few days … if Bailey lets them come with him."

"Is Bailey the type of female to be bitter?"

"Not at all. She's cool, people—sweet, kind-hearted, and thoughtful. I was surprised Cleophus dealt with her like that. She's clean-cut and respectable. She's not the type of female you would see in the club every weekend; hell, she's like you when it comes to clubbing."

"How did they meet?" I probed.

"Where the truth came out today."

"Oh. Did you meet someone there that day as well?" I voiced with a raised eyebrow.

As he cleared his throat, Fabian looked at me and said, "Bailey's cousin, Ana. Without a doubt, I knew what was going to happen between Ana and me. She was going to get the dick for a month or two, and I was going to toss her ass back to the streets."

Laughing, I replied, "So, did it go down like that?"

"Just like that. No strings attached."

"Was she present today?"

"Yep."

"And y'all didn't speak to each other?"

"Nope, she dislikes me," he chuckled before continuing, "She thought her pussy and mouth game was going to have me going past my two months mark. I had already told her I wasn't into that relationship shit unless it came down to one person. She acted like she didn't hear me the first time I said it, so I had to break it down to her who really had my heart, and why no one could ever be by my side in that manner."

"Was Ana at least relationship worthy?"

Nodding, Fabian replied, "Hell yes."

"And not one single time did you want to be in a relationship with her?"

Staring me in the eyes, he shook his head and slowly and sincerely spoke, "Not one fucking single time. I wanted who I have now. I fucked them and let them go, but I told them what was up from the jump. I had no room in my heart for another woman because someone extraordinary had already filled up the space in it. The first time you and I slept together was the first time I had ever had some pussy raw."

"Hold up, you've never had raw sex before me? You gotta be kidding?" I stated, shocked and turned on.

"I'm dead ass serious. You are the first woman I've ever lain with and not used a condom. I didn't see the need to do so; you are who I want to spend the rest of my life with. I want to give you babies. Why would I strap up, knowing what you mean to me?"

Before I knew it, I shoved him on the bed and climbed on top of him. I was no longer exhausted; I was ready to slut and be slutted out. I attacked Fabian's body with my mouth and hands in the freakiest and passionate way as I stripped him out of his clothing.

"Oh, so this is how you gonna do me?" he laughed, looking at me.

"Am I being too rough, sir?" I sassily spoke, dropping his garments onto the floor.

"No, ma'am. Have your way with me, milady," he spoke, chuckling.

Fabian didn't laugh for long. His dick was deep down my throat. His hands threw up gang signs as his toes curled. My poor, handsome best friend turned fiancé's body trembled as he moaned my name, all the while poorly glaring at me. Little did he know, those eyes and his body's reaction to what I was doing turned me on. Truthfully, I was an undercover freak; however, I never acted on my obsession with being extremely nasty in the bedroom. As of now, everything I wanted to do and try, I was going to because I had the one I always wanted to get super nasty with.

Tired of the usual sucking dick position, I slowly slid my mouth off my man and said, "Okay. So, we are going to try something new. Cool?"

"Shidd, I'm with it," he voiced as I grabbed his wrists, pulling him forwards.

"Remember the days we used to be wild when dancing?"

With a smile on his face, he replied, "The days when your legs would be in the air, and you shook that ass?"

"Yes!" I exclaimed.

"And what exactly will be my job, Nana?" he questioned curiously.

"The same as back then. Don't drop me."

"Never," he sexily voiced.

"Good. Are you ready?"

"Yes."

As he stood, tall and firm, I cleared my throat before approaching my naked man. What I was about to do, I had never done before. While Fabian planted his hands firmly on my waist and lifted me in the air, I slowly started to turn my body upside down. Of course, Fabian aided in the swift move. Grabbing his lengthy tool, I licked my lips and planted my feet on his shoulders. As I slid further down his body, I felt Fabian's knees buckle.

"My God," he moaned.

"Fabian, I feel your knees shaking. Please, please focus on the task at hand," I voiced, jacking his dick.

"Guh, you want me to focus, but you are upside down and finna suck the skin off a nigga's dick," he stated in a tone that had me laughing.

Getting myself together, I said a small prayer before I licked the head.

"Jesus," he groaned.

It's now or never, girl, I thought while I toyed around with the head of his dick.

Within a flash, I began to suckle the scrumptious penis and fondle his balls. Plenty of salivae flooded my mouth as I moaned and ground. The more dick I slid into my mouth, the more I became turned on. I had a thing for seeing his dick disappear and then reappear.

"Good gotdamn, Nana," Fabian whimpered as fingers dug into my waist.

Sucking and blowing on the head of his penis just right caused the pussy pleaser to grow. My oral sex skills intensified the more I stopped thinking and began to really enjoy being in an interesting position. Before I knew it, I was doing the nasty things I had envisioned doing to him many years ago. I went from twisting my head, moaning, and gobbling the dick to spitting on it and deep throating him. Switching things up a bit, I slowly and carefully slid my teeth from the base of his penis towards the head of his meat. Slowly and passionately, I inhaled the thick mushroom-shaped head into my mouth. Fabian became extremely weak as he groaned my name repeatedly.

"I can't take it, Nana," he moaned, his right leg on the verge of giving out.

It would've been common sense for me to stop, but I didn't. I couldn't carry on with my loving until I had some of the final prize in my belly as the rest splash on my face.

As I worked my hands and mouth just right, Fabian howled, "Ooou shiii, Nana. I'm fina cum."

With a wicked smile on my face, I continued on with my mission. Feeling the warm liquid skeet into my mouth, I swallowed as I removed his penis, allowing the rest to splash on my face.

"What the fuckkk," he moaned, legs shaking as if he was a fawn.

"You can lay back now," I told him.

"Good God, Nana," he breathlessly spoke, laying on the bed.

"What?" I voiced, enjoying his sperm drenching down my face.

Shaking his head, Fabian replied, "Nothing, baby. Nothing."

With two of my fingers, I swiped a glob of semen and sucked it off my fingers.

"Oh, my fucking goodness. You freaky freaky," he spoke in awe.

"I am. I am," I cooed, gazing into his eyes.

Once I had the rest of his protein shake off my face, I sauntered towards the bathroom. After cleaning my face and brushing my teeth, I stripped out of my clothing. Eager to sashay back into our room, I walked out of the bathroom, only to be greeted by my rejuvenated guy. There was a particular spark in his eyes that caused the corners of my mouth to turn upwards. Fabian was up to something, and I couldn't wait to find out what it was.

Placing his hand around my neck, he pushed me into the bathroom, up against the sink. There was no room for me to wiggle.

"You see, you ain't the only one on that freaky shit. So, um, let me see how wet I can get you," he spoke with a smug expression on his handsome face.

Hand still around my neck, Fabian savagely spread my legs and slipped a finger into my pretty kitty. He had a pleasant expression on his face as he softly fingered and thumb my clit. He continued that motion for a while before spicing things up tremendously. My breathing became erratic. My limbs grew weak.

"Fabian," I softly cooed as my eyes fluttered.

"What?" he spoke through clenched teeth, all the while hitting my G-Spot and applying pressure to my neck.

"Damn it now, Fabiannn," I whimpered, trying to fuck his fingers.

"Don't do no moving, Nana. I got this," he voiced provocatively before biting his bottom lip.

Six more taps to my G-Spot resulted in my body becoming too aroused; my cannon was ready to bust. I lost mobility in my limbs. If it wasn't for Fabian being so close to me, I would've collapsed on the ground.

"Let that shit go, Nana," he sternly voiced, glaring into my eyes.

"I don't want to," I whined. It felt just that damn good.

"I said to let it go," he loudly replied, fingering me faster and applying more pressure to my neck.

With rolling eyes, I held on as long as I could. The fight not to cease the amazing feeling was at an all-time high. That's until he pressed his body on mine, resulting in me leaning on the sink. The position was so uncomfortable, yet what he was doing to my body was worth it.

"Fabiannn!" I screamed, body shaking uncontrollably.

"Fuck all that screaming and calling my name shit, let that motherfucka go, NaTashia," he said through clenched teeth.

"I don't … I don't… Ohhh," I whimpered. Fabian was on the brink of getting the best of me, and I didn't want him to.

"See you hard-headed as fuck, but I got yo' ass, though," he chuckled, forcing me further onto the sink.

In the most uncomfortable position ever, I had to figure out a way to become comfortable. The more I wiggled, the more faucet pressed against the lower half of my back. I never found comfort because of Fabian's barks for me to place my legs behind my head.

"Them bitches won't work," I spoke oddly, causing him to laugh.

"Guh, put them legs behind your head," he voiced, finger fucking my pussy wonderfully.

With the little will I had, I was able to place my legs behind my head. I had no idea what I was getting myself into, but it wasn't long before I understood why he chose the bathroom. The tall motherfucker had an advantage over my five-foot-five frame.

"Oh my god, Fabian! You better not! You better not but your mouth on my pussy!

Especially when I'm in this uncomfortable position," I moaned loudly as he eyed my girl, all the while licking his lips.

While applying light pressure to my neck, Fabian beat up my G-Spot with his finger tricks. Shortly afterward, his mouth latched onto my pretty kitty. Instantly, my mind and body were on another level. The fantastic and fulfilling sensations rippled through my body was phenomenal. I had never experienced anything of this nature with Joseph. My wetness stirred about within my pink walls before cascading into my butt crack. I sensed my vocal cords getting ready to create a symphony like no other. I observed Fabian fingering and sucking my soul away from my body. Tears streamed down my face as I had no control over my violently shaking frame. I was on the brink of having an orgasm, the first of its kind. I was sure Fabian knew because his eyes told me so.

In between my pussy and asshole, I felt the pressure from his pinky finger, which resulted in me helplessly moaning, "I can't hold it anymore, Fabian. I... I can't."

With his fingers occupying my pretty kitty and massaging the perineum area, Fabian removed his hand from my neck only to lift up my ass.

"Baby, I'm cumming hard, right fucking now!" I loudly hollered.

Without a moment's hesitation, my fine man shoved his face in my squirting pussy. Not one time did he stop fingering me as he devoured me. After I had the best orgasm ever, my body didn't relax; it was still amped. Several more taps on my G-Spot resulted in me cumming.

Removing his wet face from my girl, he laughed, "That cannon still busting, huh?"

With fluttering eyes, I tried to nod; however, a high powered moan escaped my mouth. Fabian's face caught the third wave of my juices. He shook his head and growled in my pussy, sending a series of coos and moan flying through the bathroom.

"I love you. I love you. I love youuu," I sang as tears rapidly cascaded down my face.

As my body relaxed against the sink, Fabian removed his wet face and fingers from my girl, only to insert his thick and long penis into its home. Fabian wore my nutty pussy and voice box out; throughout the ordeal, I was one moaning, sweet-everything talking female. I wasn't prepared for the man who stared in my face, smiling and shoving dick deep into my pink walls. I wasn't ready for the sexual beast I had unleashed. I thought he was the one who had to be prepared for me to saddle up; it was me. Fabian fucked me as if I owed him something expensive.

Face to face, pulling my hair and fucking the shit out of me, Fabian said, "You want me to tone it down a notch, Nana?"

I couldn't answer his question with a yes or no answer, but I gave him an answer nonetheless when I said, "That's my spot, Fabian. That's my motherfucking spot. Fuck meee!"

"Say no more," he rapidly replied before parting my lips with his tongue, placing his hand around my neck, and drilling my leaky girl.

As my pleasure noises escaped my mouth, Fabian's old way of talking appeared as he savagely dicked me down. Whispering in my ear, he said, "I'mma make sure you ain't worth a damn tomorrow. I'mma make sure you know who should've always had you. I'mma make yo' ass pay fo' leavin' me an' not comin' back 'til seventeen motherfuckin' years later. I'm gon' make sure everybody knows that I been in this pussy. Do you fuckin' understand what I'm sayin', Nana?"

As he angrily glared at me, I weakly hissed, "Yesss."

Chapter Fourteen

Fabian

Sunday, December 22nd

On this day, fifteen years ago, I lost my mother to breast cancer. I was indeed a lost soul and didn't want anyone around me except Auntie Marilyn, June Bug, and Cleophus. Badly, I wished NaTashia would've been by my side as I dealt with the grief. Instead, I placed three pounds of weed and a liquor bottle by my side once the others left me.

The following year and many more after, I would shut down a few days close to the day she passed away. With plenty of pre-rolled blunts and a bottle of liquor wouldn't be far as I vibed to the only song that made it easier to deal with her passing, Harold Melvin & The Blue Notes "I Miss You". This year I didn't have the worst case of the blues. Still, I was saddened but not like I had been during the prior years. The one I loved dearly was the reason for that. She made the second most horrible day of my life bearable.

NaTashia sat in Bessie's passenger seat as the speaker knockers bumped, Harold Melvin & The Blue Notes "I Miss You". While she held my hand, I sang the song as tears slipped down my face. Severely, I wished my number one girl was living to witness the upcoming union between Nana and me. Badly, I needed my mother present to tell me how proud of me she was and that she was glad I finally got the one I needed in my life.

As I turned into the cemetery, like I had done many years prior, I started the song over and turned up the volume. In my head, Momma would hear me coming and smile. In my nice-sized head, she would be in her grave cussing me out for bumping my speaker knockers so loudly. When she was living, a few weeks after she had given me the keys to Bessie, I had placed a set of speakers in the car. Every afternoon, I would rattle her nerves by pulling in the driveway, bumping rap music. As our teenager asses filed out of Bessie, Momma would furiously swing open the screen door and cuss my ass out. Like the ignorant fools we were, we laughed and strolled towards the house. None of us entered until we hugged and kissed my momma on the cheek. That loving woman would always have something on the stove for us to snack on. Every other Friday, she would have a gift bag waiting on the kitchen table for NaTashia. I never asked my best friend what was in the bag; I was sure it was some type of clothes or shoes Momma had gotten her since Glorianna wasn't doing right by her.

"Are you ready?" NaTashia asked as I pulled onto the grass a few feet away from my mother's grave.

Turning down the radio and opening the door, I replied, "Yes."

Grabbing the flowers from the floorboard, NaTashia opened the passenger door and stepped out. I didn't walk towards Momma's gravesite until NaTashia was close enough for me to grab her hand.

Upon arriving at our destination, NaTashia placed the flower on her grave and said, "I'm sorry I wasn't here to say my final goodbyes, Mrs. Lola. Don't think for a second I didn't love or appreciate you because I did. I'm sorry for not holding your hand like you held mine when I came into your home crying over something my mother said or did to me. Most importantly, I'm sorry for leaving our favorite guy behind. Trust and believe I won't leave him again. I'm never going to leave his side. I wish you could be here, in the flesh, to see us tie the night on Christmas Eve and see the great memories we are creating, well minus the sex. I'm very sure you don't want to see that."

Shaking my head and laughing, I said, "Really, Nana?"

"I placed a smile on your face with that comment, huh?" she stated, playfully bumping me.

Sliding my hand around her waist, I smiled. "Yes, you did."

Giving my mother's grave my undivided attention, I cleaned her headstone, all the while saying, "Momma, I finally got her. It took me a minute to have the one I was meant to be with, but the wait was worth it. Remember you told me about utter happiness and a peaceful mind? Well, I have it, and I love it. I'm determined to live and feel just as you had prayed for. I have my better half with me, and I know I can weather any storm as long as we are together. Your son is finally where he needs to be in life. Thanks to Nana, I get to be the type of male figure in two amazing kids' lives. She does the whooping, which I hate. Like most dads and male figures, all I do is pacify them and keep repeating myself. Hopefully, we will be coming back soon enough with news of a little one growing in her womb. Until next time, continue watching over the ones I love the most and me. Come see me in my dreams sometimes. I would really like that. I love you, Momma. Tell Dad I said hey, and I love him. Oh, also tell him NaTashia didn't put any more dents on Bessie."

Punching me in the arm, NaTashia laughed, "Hush up."

After we blew kisses towards my mother's grave, we strolled towards the car.

"Do you want to visit your father's grave? I'm sure we can head to Lowndes County and be back in time to finish last-minute shopping."

"Not today. We can go one day this week," I told her as I opened the car door.

"Are you sure? I can drive down there."

"Yes, I'm sure. Speaking of driving, take the wheel."

"Okay," she responded, glaring into my eyes.

"Nana, I'm okay. Just don't feel like driving. That's all," I confessed.

"Okay," she replied before sitting in the driver's seat.

After I closed the door, I skipped in front of Bessie and patted the hood. As I entered the car, NaTashia pulled away and asked, "Have you talked to Cleophus today?"

"Yep, and he's about to lose his mind. That nigga ain't stopped whining about kids' neediness, a happily prancing about Bailey, and not having Santana. Your uncle is really going through it. I fear that fool might do something stupid. You know he can't handle everyday problems the right way. If it isn't the dope game, Cleophus will lose his shits."

"That's what his ass gets. He's been sending me sad ass text messages ever since Bailey decided she wouldn't send the kids down here without her being present. If he ain't bitching about Bailey's antics of wanting to have sex with him, he's ranting and raving about Santana refusing to speak to him in public."

"Shii," I stated, shaking my head.

"Do you think he will be civil towards Santana at the wedding and reception?"

"Yes. He knows what this union means to me."

"On that day, what he going to do about Bailey and the kids?"

"He's shipping them back to Birmingham tomorrow," I replied as my cell phone rang.

Looking at the screen, I said, "Speaking of the devil."

As NaTashia zoomed out of the cemetery, I answered my partner's call. The background noise informed me it was chaotic--bickering females, crying kids, and glass or something of that nature breaking.

Quickly, I sat upright in the seat and called his name.

"Nigga, get yo' ass to my place now! Santana in this bitch wearin' Bailey's ass out! Boy, come on ova here an' come get my kids! I don' fucked up big time," he rapidly spoke before ending the call.

"Nana, go to Cleophus' crib, now," I urgently spoke before sighing heavily.

"What's going on?"

"Hurricane Santana, category five."

"Ah, shit. She can turn up like that? Why in the hell is she over there in the first place?" Nana voiced as she pressed the hazard button and mashed on the gas pedal.

"Hell yeah. Santana looks like she won't kill a fly. That damn woman shut down a club before. Cleophus didn't see the anger in her eyes until she bopped him in his eyes and nose. It took June Bug and me to pull her off his ass."

"What did he do?"

"Was smiling and chit-chatting with one of her opps."

"Jesus," she stated as my cell phone rang.

Placing my eyes on the phone, I quickly answered a call from June Bug.

"What's up?"

"Mane, where yo' ass at? This guh going ham in this bitch. She don' wore Cleophus ass out. He got all types of cartoon knots on his forehead an' face. Bailey's ass hidin' in the man cave, door locked. She beat the fuck up as well."

"We headed that way. We should be there in fifteen minutes. Where are the kids?"

"I put them in one of the rooms upstairs. I'm holdin' Junior."

As I heard Santana yelling at Cleophus, a loud thud sounded off.

"Ooh, shit," June Bug loudly voiced before saying, "Man, get yo' ass over here before she concuss this nigga."

"What the fuck was that sound?"

"If I tell yo' ass to hurry up over here before she concuss that nigga, what you think that sound was, Fabo? She popped that nigga in the face, and his head hit the livin' room wall."

Loudly, June Bug said, "A'ight, Santana, you've made yo' point. Leave that nigga alone."

"You better shut the fuck up before I get at your ass next. All you motherfuckas was smiling in my damn face knowing he was laid up with that popeyed, yella bitch!" Santana responded nastily.

"Bruh, I don't want no fucking trouble with this chick. Please come calm this situation down," he begged.

"What is she doing now?"

"Don' dragged Cleophus outside."

"Say what now?" I questioned, stunned.

"Nigga you heard me," June Bug stated.

"Mannn," I dragged out as my homie began to chuckle heartedly.

Santana was a slim-thick type of woman; Cleophus was a stocky type of dude. She stood five-foot-seven; he was five-foot-eleven. Santana participated faithfully in kickboxing and other defensive classes. Cleophus was a regular at the gym. All in all, Cleophus wasn't a match for the woman.

"Oh shit! Santana, chill, man!" June Bug spat as I heard a thud before a door opened.

I called my partner's name several times before I ceased speaking. Looking at NaTashia, I said, "You gotta get to Cleophus house faster than fifteen minutes. I need you to open the motor up in this motherfucka."

"Are you sure?" she asked, nervously.

Seeing her position of driving fast, I shook my head and said, "Pullover. I'll take the reins from here."

Quickly, on the side of the road, we swapped seats. Before she could place the seatbelt over her body, I hopped onto the road before diving onto the interstate. Cleophus lived on the south side of town, and we were on the northeastern side. While I bobbed and weaved through traffic, I placed my phone on speaker. I needed to hear what was going on in the background.

"Should I call her?" NaTashia inquired.

Shaking my head, I responded, "I'm sure her phone is nowhere around her. When she's pissed, she's pissed. No material items stand a chance against her."

"Aye, man, you need to bust through whatever cars in yo' way. Som' of Cleophus neighbors tried to pull Santana off him, but she wore their asses out too. She back pouncin' on his ass. I'on wanna pop her ass in the leg, but that's my next move, bruh. That bitch too strong fo' any of us niggas."

"Shid, if you gotta pop her as ... hit her foot. Don't shoot her in the leg; you might kill her."

Before the word 'her' settled out of my mouth good enough, a gunshot sounded off.

With a racing heartbeat, I loudly asked, "Who's shot?"

June Bug didn't respond because he was too busy hollering at Santana to put the gun down.

"Fuck!" I spat, mashing on the gas pedal and running red lights.

Thankfully, traffic wasn't heavy for the next several lights.

"June Bug, please tell me you have put Junior in his car seat or bassinet, away from the bullshit?" NaTashia asked.

Her questioned went unanswered as June Bug repeatedly hollered, "What the fuck, Santana? What the fuck!"

At the same time, NaTashia and I yelled, "What's wrong?"

"This guh don' shot Cleophus in his leg. Bruh, what the fuck you want me to do? Call the cops or take him to the E.R.," June Bug spoke in a high-pitched tone.

"Knock Santana's ass out and get Cleophus to the E.R.," I spoke through clenched teeth.

"Knock her out wit' my hands?" he inquired nervously.

"Yeah, nigga, not with the gun, fool."

"That guh don' boxed them other niggas to their knees. What the fuck you think she gon' do to me? I'm a fool, but not that much of a fool."

"Nigga, you gonna have to do what you gotta. I'm not anywhere near y'all. You gonna have to step up and handle the situation!"

"A'ight," he replied before sighing heavily.

For a while, he breathed heavily. The moment his breathing became too steady as if he was ceasing the involuntary actions of breathing, I sat upright in the seat and called his name several times. There was no doubt in my mind he was going to shoot Santana, which was going to be a problem.

"June Bug, I said don't shoot her! Knock her ass out! Do not shoot that girl, June Bug!"

Pow.

"Fuckkk!" Santana hollered in pain.

"I had too. I had to shoot her. She was standin' over Cleophus wit' the gun aimed at his head. I had to shoot her, Fabian. I had too," my partner voiced as it seemed like he was running.

Weakly, Cleophus asked, "Did you have to shoot her?"

"Bitch nigga, yeah. The girl don' whooped yo' ass all up an' through yo' shit. She popped yo' ass an' stood over you wit' a gun. What the fuck you think I was gonna do?" June Bug asked as Santana cried out in pain.

"She did what I told her to do," Cleophus stated as Santana began to loudly wail from that hot lead.

"What?" June Bug, NaTashia, and I exclaimed.

"Why you think she was here from the jump? Because I told her she could beat my ass an' possibly shot me if it would put me in her good graces."

"Are you fucking serious?" we loudly voiced as Santana's screams sent chills running through my body.

Without a moment's notice, I lifted off the gas pedal and turned off the hazard lights.

"So, you had Santana come over here an' beat yo' babies momma's ass too?" June Bug inquired as I shook my head at the foolishness I heard.

"No. She wasn't supposed to have known Bailey was in the house. Bailey's stupid ass came out the door, talkin' mad shit. That's when things got out of control," Cleophus stated as police sirens sounded off.

"Mann," I said before saying, "I'm finna hang up."

Without waiting for June Bug to respond, I ended the call.

"What in the hell goes through my Uncle's mind?" NaTashia voiced.

"That's exactly what I want to know. We will find out shortly."

Cleophus was known for doing and saying stupid shit; today's actions were the most ridiculous shit he'd ever done. He made a situation more prominent than it had to be. He fucked up. He placed his children in a heated position they should've never been in. My partner was so pressed about Santana, he didn't think about the well-being of his kids.

When we arrived on the scene, I shook my head and deeply sighed. Amongst the two officers, male and female, an ambulance, and June Bug, there was a crowd of people with their phones in their hands.

Hopping out of Bessie, I aimed towards June Bug as he talked to the female police officer. The male officer was questioning Cleophus, stupid ass.

As the female officer and June Bug walked away from each other, he looked at me and said, "Man, this shit was uncalled fo'."

"Extremely," I stated as NaTashia made her way towards Santana, who was being placed on a gurney.

"How bad is her injury, June Bug?" I inquired, observing the scene.

"I don't know. By the way she screamed, I say bad. I don' capped a lot of niggas in the knees, and none of them made the sound she did," he replied as the second ambulance pulled onto the curb.

"Now, look at his stupid ass with a hole in his damn leg," I voiced, shaking my head.

I watched NaTashia make her way back to us, shaking her head with a disappointed expression on her face.

"Niece," Cleophus said as the second set of EMT's stepped out of the work vehicle.

"What?" my woman voiced, not looking at her uncle.

"I'm sorry to ruin yo' day."

Exhaling deeply, NaTashia said, "You didn't ruin my day. You ruined the day for your children. You placed them in a bad headspace. They are too young to be dealing with this childish bullshit. You need to grow up and think of them more than you do. From what I've gathered about Santana, she isn't the type to play with. You fucked up y'all's relationship. You should've dealt with it instead of consenting to stupidity, just to be in her good graces. I'm not going to spend another damn second here. I'm going on about my business because I have fucking wedding and reception to finalize. I'll check on you when my tasks are completed."

Just like that, NaTashia walked towards Bessie as I dapped June Bug before strolling towards Cleophus.

As I shook his hand, I said, "Once you are released from the hospital, have June Bug bring your stupid ass to my crib."

"A'ight," he voiced as the medics began to prepare the fool to be loaded onto the gurney. Walking away, I overheard the police officers saying they would charge Santana with assault with a deadly weapon. Now, her life would forever be changed for the stupid action she could've left lingering in Cleophus' mouth.

§§§

At seven-thirty p.m., our home was alive and vibrant. It was a surprise seeing my cousins, all of OG Buckingham and Auntie Rebecca's children, in a positive headspace. There wasn't any evil eyeing between Orthello and me. During the wake of his father, we ditched the foolery. He sought the best course to run his father's empire, and I happily told him the best way to do it. So far, he took my advice. The crew was becoming what it should've been all along, and they respected what I had to say.

While Christmas music played, I observed the layout of my family and friends. Cleophus hobbled around on a crutch, talking shit. June Bug, Orthello, and Auntie Marilyn carried in wedding decorations, only to place them on the backyard's porch. Auntie Rebecca, NaTashia, Monique, and Sasha sat at the table, going over wedding setups and seatings. Danya, OG Buckingham and Auntie Rebecca's last child, was sitting in the far right corner of the kitchen, putting together centerpieces.

The vibe in the house damn near brought tears to my eyes. A huge smile was on my face as I glared at my family. I was sure Momma would've been proud to be amongst us.

After her father's wake, NaTashia stated she didn't want anything to do with those boujee sisters of hers; apparently, they rubbed her the wrong way. Within a few hours of us arriving home that day, the sisters came over and apologized for how they acted towards her. Shortly afterward, the sisters took their time getting to know each other. Immediately, upon meeting their niece and nephew, NaTashia's sisters fell in love with them. Later that night, their brothers came over. It was a beautiful sight to see my woman interacting with those that share the same male DNA as her.

"Boy, what yo' black butt over there 'bout to cry 'bout?" Sasha asked, causing everyone to laugh.

"I'm loving this moment. Everyone is on one accord, viewing each other as equals. We spreading love, kindness, and jokes. We are a unit," I confessed, looking amongst them.

"There he go wit' that mushy shit," June Bug and Cleophus voiced in unison, resulting in everyone, including me, to laugh.

"I swear. That nigga will pop yo' ass in a second but has the nerve to be mushy. Now, what kind of shit is that?" Danya inquired with a smile on her face.

"He's just like his Momma. Every bit of her," Auntie Rebecca voiced, Auntie Marilyn, agreeing with her.

"I remember that time Lola shot Edwin. My damn sister was talking mushy to him as she popped his ass. I didn't know whether to laugh or be fearful," Auntie Marilyn spoke loudly, causing us to gasp and ask why.

"Oh, let's not talk about the time she shot Willie in his hands," Auntie Rebecca stated, laughing.

"What?" we exclaimed.

"Hold up, Ma," Orthello loudly said before continuing, "You let Auntie Lola shoot daddy?"

"It wasn't like I let her shoot him. Hell, she talked so smoothly and calmly to him; it never crossed my mind she would shoot him. I didn't see her pull the gun out."

"Why she shot her husband and daddy?" Monique asked curiously.

"She shot Edwin because she thought he was cheating on her," Auntie Rebecca voiced.

"Was he?" I inquired.

At the same time, my aunties hollered, "Hell no. He was secretly meeting up with us because he wanted to host the perfect birthday party for her."

"I bet Auntie felt like shit when she learned the truth," Sasha stated.

Laughing, Auntie Marilyn said, "Yes, she did. Damn woman cried for a week straight behind that shit."

"Why she shot Daddy?" Orthello asked.

"Because she heard he had slapped me," Auntie Rebecca replied.

"Did he?" her children probed.

"Yep."

"An' you didn't mess him up?" Danya questioned.

"Oh, I fucked him, alright. He had a broken leg and a fractured rib behind his wondering hand."

"After they did your father in, I had to put him in his place to let him know no one fucks with us girls," Auntie Marilyn voiced, taking a seat at the table.

"What did you do?" NaTashia inquired.

As my aunties laughed and looked at each other, the suspense of knowing was at an all-time high.

"What in the hell did Auntie Marilyn do, Ma?" Vincent, the second child of Auntie Rebecca's, asked.

"That damn heifer put an entire bottle of lemon-flavored magnesium citrate in a jug of tea. The heifer even added sliced lemons to the concoction."

"Jesus," NaTashia laughed before saying, "So, not only did he have trouble walking and somewhat breathing, he had issues with using his hands. What a helluva combination when your asshole leaking, constantly."

Pointing at NaTashia, Auntie Marilyn hollered, "And that's why I did it. Oh, he was going to feel the wrath of slapping my damn sister. I made sure he knew what it was to fuck with us. A raw ass is nothing to play with."

While we laughed, Vincent said, "Daddy, never stood a chance against y'all, huh?"

"Not at all," my aunties voiced, looking at him.

"No wonder Sasha, Danya, and Monique be doing the most. It runs in their DNA," Orthello voiced, shaking his head.

Immediately, my aunties laughed and looked at my cousins. From there, many stories of how my girl cousins fucked up my male cousins. Those niggas didn't stand a chance with them. According to them, all types of pranks took place under their roof when they were teenagers. If the girls didn't get their way or the fellas didn't stand up for them when they were into with a dude, all hell would break loose.

"Danya is the most treacherous one of all!" my male cousins laughed.

"How many motors have she messed up of mine?" Vincent chuckled.

"Dude, you talkin' 'bout motors ... man, that guh used to destroy my bedroom. I mean destroy it," Orthello loudly voiced, banging on the kitchen counter.

"How many of our dogs did she turn against us?" Nick, the third child, spoke, shaking his head.

While each of them told their stories, I was amazed at my cousin's ability. She was beyond smart. At that moment, my mind started to scurry about her. She would've been a great battle consultant.

Pulling Orthello to the side, I asked, "Does Danya have a thing for the street life?"

"Yeah. Why, you ask?"

"From what I gathered, she's the person you have over battle consultant. It seems she learns people's strengths and weaknesses quickly. She can bring a motherfucker to their knees, all the while looking innocent. Also, she could fill the position of learning about those you conduct business with."

"Damn, I didn't see her abilities like that. In that case, I need to promote her fast."

"What you had her doing?"

"Money launderin'."

"Bruh, that sounds like something Sasha could be doing. That woman is great with moving money around."

"How do you know that?" he inquired, shocked.

"Who you think gave me the insight to move money around?" I chuckled.

"What else can you tell me that'll help me out?"

"A whole lot," I voiced as the front door opened.

Instantly, the house became quiet as everyone's eyes were placed on Glorianna. As she strolled through my cozy home, she had the ugliest expression on her face.

"Don't come in here wit' that Grinch attitude, Glorianna," Cleophus voiced, from the far end of the kitchen.

"You don't tell me what the hell to do, stupid little boy. Better worry about that skeezer who you let shoot you," Glorianna voiced.

"What you ain't finna do is come into my home and not speak to a soul or act like you have the right to move about in a certain way. Like your brother said, don't come in here with that attitude," I sternly said, eyeing her.

Rolling her eyes, Glorianna nastily spoke to everyone. Not a soul responded.

"What are you doing here, Momma?" NaTashia inquired, not looking back.

"Hmm," Auntie Rebecca voiced, which caused NaTashia and me to look at her.

As Auntie Rebecca turned towards the kitchen walk-in, everyone stopped doing their tasks. Quickly, I braced myself for what was about to go down.

"I came to see if this little fairytale of yours is really happening," Glorianna chuckled.

The look upon Auntie Rebecca's face shown she was going to do something.

Sighing sharply, NaTashia said, "Momma, you might want to leave. I'm not responsible for what happens."

"And what the fuck that supposed to mean, little girl?" Glorianna shouted, stepping closer into the kitchen.

Before NaTashia could open her mouth, Glorianna did what she did best. Embarrass and hurt my woman's feelings. As usual, Cleophus and I came to NaTashia's defense. Before we could get the rest of the words out of our mouths, Auntie Rebecca coughed. That was our cue to shut up, which we did.

By the time Glorianna finished ruining my baby's spirit, NaTashia had hopped to her feet and hurtfully said, "You can't go a week without hurting me, huh? Does that bring pleasure to your bitter soul? Does it make you feel good to belittle me? Do you sleep well at night knowing I respect you enough not to hurt you like you do me? Does it bring you fucking pleasure to know I honor God enough not to break a few of His ten commandments?"

Loudly, Auntie Rebecca said, "NaTashia, sit down and don't say another word to that bitch. Do not, and I mean, do not let her steal your joy and peace. Don't let her get the best of you with her words. You, of all people, know what she speaks isn't true. I see why my husband placed Cleophus under his wing. Now, I understand why my nephew decided to side with Cleophus in the streets. I truly understand why he used to beat on her. That old bitter bitch doesn't deserve to have you in her life."

The expression on Glorianna and Auntie Rebecca's children's faces were priceless. Today, they learned a lot about NaTashia's past.

Standing, my auntie said, "You are one poor excuse of a mother. You know what, you aren't a mother; you is a mammie. The way you talk to your daughter is a fucking shame. She didn't ask to be on this earth. You and my husband's dealings got her here. Never should a woman fault her child for what didn't go right in her life. In this short amount of time, I've gotten to know NaTashia; she's one splendid, gifted, and intelligent being. She's super well-mannered, thoughtful, kind, and loving. How dare you come to her as if she's anything less? I'm not going to tell you things about your child that you already know. However, I'm going to tell you something that you must consider the next time you fix your damn mouth to speak to her in any way other than respectable. As you know, I'm one of those females many old heads in our age group fear. I am the type of woman who will shoot you while you are drinking tea on your front porch with your neighbors. I'm sure you've heard of me from neighborhood talks, once I aim … I don't miss. I've never missed a fucking head I shot at. Take that as the final warning,

Glorianna. You will *not* destroy my nephew and my soon to be niece in law's happy moment. Or should I say ... you will not destroy my step-daughter's wedding nuptials?"

The silence throughout the house was eerie. Everyone glared between the women; I was sure they pondered what Glorianna's comeback was. However, I knew there wasn't going to be a comeback message. Glorianna wasn't dumb for real.

"Can somebody pick up that microphone from Rebecca's feet?" Cleophus laughed, resulting in the majority of us chuckling.

As Glorianna turned on her heels and exited our home, NaTashia stood and sadly said, "I can't do this."

"NaTashia," Cleophus and I called in unison as she walked away.

"I'm not in a talking mood," she spoke, strutting down the hallway, wiping her face.

Immediately, all of NaTasia's siblings called her name as they followed behind her.

As I sat in the chair my woman was in, Auntie Rebecca said, "She's going to come back with a smile on her face. Those knucklehead children of mine are going to put her head in the right space.

Trust me, they will. Once they come up here, your task is going to be hard."

With a raised eyebrow, I asked, "What task?"

"To keep Orthello from killing Glorianna, tonight. One thing about that nigga, he doesn't play about his sisters. Yes, he just learned and accepted NaTashia as his sister. That doesn't mean a damn thing. He's falling in love with being her big brother. Just like he moves hell and heaven for Danya, Sasha, and Monique, he will do the same for NaTashia."

Thirty minutes later, Auntie Rebecca's words came true. It took a lot for me to keep Orthello's head in the game. He was fuming with anger. He didn't understand why a woman could be so cruel to her child. At that moment, I was positive NaTashia told them how she was mistreated by her mother.

After an hour of talking him off the killing ledge, we returned to the singing, chair dancing, and busy people. It was as if Glorianna hadn't appeared, almost destroying our spirit.

As the time approached for our company to leave, two police officers and a man of the cloth were on the porch. One of the officers knocked on the screen door. Being the man of the house, I invited them in. Upon everyone seeing the chaplain, the house became extremely quiet as all eyes were locked onto them. After the pleasantries sounded from our mouths, they told me who they were looking for.

Upon nodding, I led the way to the kitchen. Once they arrived in the cluttered kitchen, filled with plates and wedding items, the chaplain began to speak to Cleophus. The chaplain could barely get Santana's last name out of his mouth before a gutwrenching sob escaped his mouth. As we gasped at the news of Santana's death during surgery, the mood in the house was dark and gray.

As NaTashia rushed to his side, June Bug poorly held up our buddy as he cried for the woman he loved.

"The doctor said it was a simple surgery, and she would be fine after he fixed her knee. What the hell happened?" he cried, glaring into the chaplain's face.

"There was a complication," the chaplain voiced as two knocks sounded on the screen door.

Walking away from the kitchen, holding in tears, my knees buckled as I saw two officers and a chaplain.

As I opened the screen door, I sighed heavily before saying, "Yes?"

"Is there a NaTashia Wells here?" one of the officers asked.

Nodding, I replied, "Yes, she is."

"If this is about Santana Moore, we've been notified," I replied, glaring into each of their faces.

"I'm sorry, sir, but we didn't come here for that person," the female chaplain stated before continuing, "May we come in, please?"

Sighing deeply, I said, "Yes."

As Cleophus, June Bug, and my phone sounded off, I walked into the kitchen with the officers and chaplain behind me.

"My God. Who is it now?" Auntie Marilyn voiced sadness on her face.

"NaTashia, baby, come here," I softly said as she held tightly onto her crying uncle.

Staring at me with a tear-stained face, NaTashia loudly said, "Not now, Fabian. I'm over here consoling my uncle. I know you see that."

At that moment, everyone in the room knew who the second chaplain was here to see.

"Mann, don't tell me my sister is dead too," Cleophus cried while continuing, "Yeah, she was messed up, but gotdamn she is my sister."

"She ain't dead, boy! They are here because of Santana. There is a mix-up, and they sent out two sets of people to notify the next of kin," NaTashia spoke while crying and barely hanging onto her uncle.

As the female chaplain walked towards, NaTashia softly talking to her, my woman cried. We learned Glorianna ran her car off the Alabama River's bridge, resulting in immediate death.

Once the officers and chaplains left, everyone was stuck in place. My partner cried as he held tightly to his sad niece. I didn't know what to say to either of them about Glorianna. She didn't leave an impression on me that would've caused me to show grave sympathy for her. Yet, I told them that I was sorry for their loss. As far as Santana, her death hit me. I knew her well enough for tears to slide down my face as I dropped in front of my partner, holding his trembling hand.

In a hurtful tone, June Bug stuttered, "I'll understand if you want to seek revenge, Cleo—"

Angrily, Cleophus yelled, "Bitch, I ain't seeking revenge. You did what any homie of mine should've done. The blame doesn't sit wit' you nigga. It sits wit' me! If I hadn't kept it one-hunnid wit' her 'bout my kids, she would still be livin'. I'm the one at fault. I'm the one who put the pressure on her to turn into a beast, so I could have her back in my life. It's my fuckin' fault! I did this to her! I killed her! I murdered the one I needed to spend the rest of my life with!"

As June Bug sat on the floor beside Cleophus, he grabbed his hand at the same time I grabbed NaTashia's hand and placed a kiss on the back of it.

"We gonna get through this together like we get through everythin' else," June Bug voiced as I didn't take my eyes off my woman.

Chapter Fifteen

NaTashia

Christmas Eve

The past two days were hectic. I had to deal with a lot. Santana's parents were nasty and rude. They refused to exchange numbers so that I could attend her funeral. They wanted information as to why their child was shot. No one told them why; the less said, the better.

Being the respectable daughter I was, I took over the reins of putting together funeral plans for Momma. I was beyond overwhelmed, resulting in Fabian telling me he felt it was best to push our date back. I declined. Our date had meaning, and I wasn't going to settle for any date just to grieve my mother. Yes, she was my mother, but she wasn't going to get the upper hand. She wasn't going to be the highlight of my life. It wasn't like I was the highlight of hers.

Yesterday afternoon, I had the pleasure of learning that I wasn't Momma's beneficiary of nothing; Uncle Paul was. He was to receive the house, car, and insurance policy. She even stated in her will, he would be the one to be over her funeral preparations. While laughing at the foolish woman, I contacted Uncle Paul. The man was a joke, just like his sister was. By the time I got off the phone with him, I was one stunned woman. Uncle Paul stated he wasn't going to give his sister a funeral; he would cremate her. He was hell-bent on not wasting unnecessary money to put her in the ground. As far as her house and car, he was going to sell it. When I told Cleophus and Fabian, they were shocked. After that discussion, I resumed being focused on my nuptial day and the reception with the help from Auntie Marilyn, Rebecca, and my sisters. I was hell-bent on not worrying about anything I couldn't control.

"Are you ready for tonight, sissy?" Monique asked as she, Danya, and Sasha kicked off their shoes and climbed in the bed.

"Yes." I smiled.

"Is there anything we need to focus on before we jazz up that hair and slay your makeup?" Sasha asked, looking at me.

"The only thing y'all are responsible for is to keep me company and cease my friend from thinking about Santana. Anything related to the wedding, Rebecca and the other ladies can take care of that. I just want to sit in this room before it's time for me to get dolled up," I told them as I grabbed the remote control.

As I powered on the TV, Danya asked, "Are any of your other family members coming to the wedding?"

"Yes, it's a small crowd, though. The others heard wind of it, and they are royally pissed that I'm going to continue on with it despite what happened. The other half pissed because they didn't receive an invite," I replied, flipping through the TV channels.

"Well, fuck them. Do not let them ruin your day," Sasha stated.

"Trust, I'm not. It's not like they were there for me anyway. So, their feelings don't matter to me."

Silence overcame the room as Monique looked at me apologetically and said, "That day in the store, when I learned who you were, I never apologized for how I acted or what I said. I know I came off as a total bitch, and I'm truly sorry for making you feel anything less than worthy of being a part of our lives."

Grabbing her hand, I smiled and said, "I humbly and proudly accept your apology."

After we hugged, the ladies asked about our honeymoon and who would care for Maxon and Angel.

"Of course, Fabian's ass wanted to do the most for our honeymoon. Since I don't have a passport, we had to purchase an expedited one. So, for the first part of our honeymoon, we will be in Hawaii for four days. The next one will be in Bora Bora."

Excitedly, my sisters said, "Now, you better take plenty of pictures while y'all are in Bora Bora."

"No doubt. Fabian already purchased a camera for that trip."

Knock. Knock.

"Come in," I said, looking at the door.

"Mommy! Aunties!" Angel happily voiced as she ran into the room, shaking her freshly braided hair.

"Ohh, look at you. You are super gorgeous, Angel," I praised my little mini-me.

"Thank you," she quickly stated before hugging each of her aunties.

"Where's your brother?" I asked, ogling my pretty girl.

"He's talking to Auntie Marilyn and Mrs. Rebecca," she quickly voiced before continuing, "Momma, some girl in the barbershop was staring at my brother and smiling. I think he likes her too because he kept looking at the girl."

As we probed for more information about this mystery girl, Angel climbed into my lap and said, "She was pretty, Momma."

"She was?"

"Yep," she replied, nodding.

Giggling, I said, "Tell your brother I said to come here, sweetheart."

"No, ma'am. I was told by Fabian that you can't see him or Maxon ... not tonight."

"Fabian's here?" I asked, blushing as butterflies floated in the pit of my stomach.

"Yes, ma'am. You have to stay in here until they are gone. That's what Fabian said," she voiced as my phone rang.

Grabbing my device off the nightstand, I smiled as I stared at my best friend's name. Quickly, I answered the phone.

"Hello there, you," I cooed.

"Eww, Momma, what's wrong with your voice?" Angel asked, frowning.

As my sisters and I laughed, Fabian chuckled in my ear. "She surely has a lot of questions. You didn't tell me she's very observant and asks a million questions before you answer the first question."

"Ah, I forgot that key detail. What are you doing here?"

"I forgot something."

"Is it in the room?"

"No. I moved it out of the room and put it in the man cave."

"Okay. Are you in the man cave now?"

"No, I'm sitting in the front room."

"Do you have what you came for?"

"Yes."

"Okay."

Lovingly, Fabian said, "I missed holding you last night."

"Same this way. How was the bachelor party?"

Laughing, he replied, "Them niggas showed the fuck out. I swear I kept my hands to myself, but those cousins of mine were turned up. Cleophus couldn't get his mind right to attend, and I understood. It felt weird not having him by my side. Honestly, I couldn't fully enjoy myself because he was on my mind.

"I spent a great deal of time last night talking to him. He's messed up mentally. I pray nothing else foolish creeps across his mind. I really feel the need to keep a close eye on him."

Sighing heavily, he genuinely voiced, "I feel the same way. I really want him to come stay with us for a few days. Would you be okay with that?"

"Of course."

"On a serious and honest tip, do you really want to get married tonight? I know the past couple of days have been rough. If it's too much, we can always push our date back, Nana."

I looked at the phone and hung it up.

Shortly afterward, I yelled, "Mention something else about me pushing our wedding date back. I promise you I'm going to tear the top off your head, Fabo! Have your ass back at this house at eight-fifteen p.m.! Do I make myself clear?"

He laughed for a while before shouting, "Crystal clear, baby. Crystal clear. I wouldn't miss it for anything in the world!"

"Good!"

"Hey, Momma!" Maxon screamed.

"Hey, son. I missed you last night!"

"I missed you as well! We gotta go! See you tonight!"

"See you tonight!"

Peeping her head into the room, Auntie Marilyn winked at us and said, "Cupcake, are you ready to go?"

With a massive smile on her face, Angel said, "Yes, ma'am. I will have the front seat all to myself."

"Sorry, doll face, you won't. I have dibs on that front seat," Rebecca replied, smiling as she stepped into our line of vision.

Rubbing her hands together, Angel said, "Oh, Mrs. Rebecca, I'm fine with that as well."

"Girl, why are you rubbing your hands like that and eyes have dollar signs in them?" Danya laughed.

"Because she knows what it means when I sit in the front seat, and it's just us girls," Rebecca replied as Marilyn laughed.

Shaking my head and smiling, I said, "It's Christmas Eve. What could y'all possibly be buying?"

"For us to know, and you to find out later," Auntie Marilyn winked before walking off.

As we laughed at that character of a woman, Rebecca extended her hand. After telling me she would see me later and issued out her hugs, the duo left. Upon the front door closing, the sound of peace and quiet floated through the house. Once Danya yawned, the rest of us did.

"Can we go to sleep for a little while? We've been up all night as if we are young," Sasha voiced, outstretching on the bed.

"Yes, we can. I need a nap because I'm sure I won't see sleep until after Christmas," I replied as we began to spread out in the bed.

As my sisters found sleep quickly, I had a smile on my face as I thought of how my life turned out in less than four weeks. Since I returned to Alabama, I had my first sleepover with females, my sisters. I had found a family that had my back more than the ones I'd known all of my life. My children were happy with the new additions in our lives. Everyone was at peace with each other. This was indeed the best holiday season I had ever had, minus the deaths. I was beyond thankful and blessed that I returned to the one place I had escaped.

§§§

Ever since I strolled into our backyard, tears streamed down my face. The wedding party was beautiful, just like the decorations. The flower girl, Angel, was stunning in her dress; the ring bearer, Maxon, was a handsome little something. My sisters' looked radiant in their dresses, which they had to purchase at the last minute. The groomsmen were handsome as ever; just like my sisters' had to buy their items at the last minute, so did my brothers. Due to the crutches, Cleophus couldn't give me away, so he agreed for Orthello to walk me towards my fiancé. The best man, Cleophus, put on his best look. Everyone knew he was grieving, but he tried his best to put on a good show. Even I had to suck it up because I knew Santana wouldn't want me grieving her on my special day. I really wished she was alive to be apart of the blissful union between Fabian and me.

When I stepped in front of the groom, tears cascaded down his handsome face. I tried everything in my power to cease the tears from dripping down my beautifully makeup filled face.

As the wedding officiant spoke during our ceremony, my heart leaped with joy as my soul was at peace. I had chosen the perfect mate to be the provider and protector of our household. I was finally with the one that made my world better.

Our unique wedding vows had the small crowd wiping their faces and awing. Of course, my crybaby best friend damn near boohooed as I spoke my vows to him. Fabian's vows were the reason I was going to have him sneak us into our room for a brief session of his sperm sliding down my throat.

Oh, yes, we are about to wrap this up, I thought as this officiant looked at us and smiled.

"Fabian and NaTashia, you have expressed your love to one another through the commitment and promises you have just made. It is with these in mind that I pronounce you husband and wife. You have kissed a thousand times, maybe more. But today, the feeling is new. No longer simply partners and best friends, you have become husband and wife and can now seal the agreement with a kiss. Today, your kiss is a promise to love and honor each other for the rest of your days. Fabian, you may kiss your bride."

In a swift yet gentle move, Fabian pulled me close to him and softly said, "Give me those beautiful, juicy lips, Nana."

Since our kids were in the crowd, we kept it sweet and short. Thankful for the many cheers, I whispered in his ear, "We need to visit our room for a brief second, husband."

"It'll be my pleasure, wife." He smiled as we proceeded to walk towards the back door.

As we neared the back door, from behind us, Rebecca loudly said, "All right, y'all, it's time to head to the reception area."

Approaching me, Danya smiled, "I'm so happy for you, sister. I can't wait until you see how we've set up your reception area. You are going to love it. Momma went all out. She acted like she was the damn bride."

"Thank you, and I know I will love it. She's exquisite down to the fingernail polish she wears," I replied as our guests congratulated us on their way out of the door.

"Well, let me get going. I need to change and set up a few more things before Momma's backyard becomes too packed," Danya stated as we embraced.

After we saw everyone safely to their cars, I closed and locked the door. As I turned to face my husband, he gently pushed me against the door frame and glared into my eyes.

Rubbing my cheeks, he sincerely spoke, "Tonight, you've given me the best Christmas present I've ever had. You have truly made me the proudest man standing on this earth, Nana.

I'm looking forward to growing old with you. You were made just for me."

With teary eyes, I placed my hand behind his head and pushed it forward. As we stared into each other's eyes, I parted his lips with my tongue. Our kiss was so intense and hot, it heated my core. Instantly, I began to massage the nape of his neck as his hands roamed my backside.

"I'll never get tired of kissing and touching on you, Nana," he voiced against my lips.

"As I will never get tired of feeling your hands and kisses upon my body," I replied, unbuckling his belt and unzipping his pants.

"Oh, so we going to do this right before our reception?" he chuckled.

Provocatively eyeing him, I responded, "Now, you know how we get down. We won't have time for that, but we will have time for you to bust down my throat."

As I dropped to my knees, Fabian's eyes fluttered as he said, "Good God. Team no sleep when we get back, right?"

With his dick in my hand, I said, "Team no motherfucking sleep when we get back, Fabo."

Chapter Sixteen

Fabian

Christmas Day

As they jumped up and down on our bed, Maxon and Angel happily and excitedly screamed, "Merry Christmas! Get up! Get up! Breakfast is ready!"

"Whoa, whoa, stop jumping on the bed," NaTashia voiced lowly.

Wiping my crusty eyes as my head pounded, I smiled, "Merry Christmas."

"We are getting out of bed now. Wait for us in the living room, please," NaTashia yawned, stretching.

"Yes, ma'am. Please don't take long. Santa has left us a lot of gifts," Angel beamed.

Acting as if I was shocked, I replied, "Oh, did he really? Y'all must've been mighty nice, huh?"

In unison, they replied, "Yes, we have. We even called our sister and brother and wished them and their mother a Merry Christmas."

These kids are so amazing and thoughtful, I thought as NaTashia smiled, "That's so sweet of you two."

"Mrs. Liddia told us to tell you to give her a call when you can," Angel voiced.

"Okay."

"But Momma, can it be after we've opened our presents?" Maxon inquired.

"Yes, son," she replied.

"Yesss!" they hissed before they ran out of our room.

Rolling over to face my wife, I said, "They are the best kids ever. We are lucky to be in their lives."

"I agree," she responded, glaring into my face.

"On another note, somebody still doesn't know how to handle liquor, huh?"

Placing her head on my chest, NaTashia replied, "Shit no. Those damn siblings of mine have bellies like a goat. Every time I turned around, they were shoving shot cups my way. I really don't think I'm going to be worth a damn today."

Rubbing her face and glaring into her eyes, I responded, "I'll breathe life back into you, just like you did me. Lean on me today and any other day for strength."

Cupping my face, NaTashia softly planted a kiss on my lips before saying, "My knight in shining armor."

"Always," I stated as her cell phone rang.

Rolling over to retrieve her device, I flipped the covers off me. As I planted my feet on the ground and stretched, NaTashia answered her phone.

"Hello."

While I walked around the front of the bed, she said, "Cleophus, that house was never any of my business. She left it to Uncle Paul. I'm done with the entire thing. I'm not going to stress over any of it, and I suggest you don't either. It's a waste of time."

Slipping into the bathroom, I closed the door and rehashed past events. The past few days were unbelievable. Some things were great, while others were a disgrace. From beyond the grave, Glorianna tried her best to break my woman's spirit. Being the strong woman she was, NaTashia gave it to the higher being and lived her life the way she was supposed to—only focusing on the things she could change.

Just like her uncle took Santana's death hard, so did NaTashia. She would skip out on conversations when Cleophus, June Bug, and I talked about the old days with Santana. NaTashia would say a few things before growing quiet and distant. My woman finally found someone she could be friends with, and just like that, her friend was gone. NaTashia never had to deal with the death of a friend before, and I tried my best to help her through it. During the day, she was strong and smiling; yet, her eyes would let me know she wasn't entirely happy. At night, when the kids were sleep, NaTashia would disappear into the bathroom and cry. She thought I didn't know because of the running water and music playing, but I knew.

My homie, Cleophus, was all over the place. Since the death of his love, he's been laying low. He didn't discuss any street business; June Bug and I handled that. We didn't know when he would be right again; however long it took, we were going to be by his side and pull his weight.

Out of all the sadness, happiness, peace, and joy surrounded us. I was beyond thankful and glad to see NaTashia creating memories with her siblings. I loved seeing them together; I love how overprotective Vincent, Orthello, and Nick had become. I valued what they had: a sibling bond.

During our reception, which was an over the top occasion, I had a little breakdown. For me, family was everything, and we had that. Yet, I needed my parents to be present in the flesh. I wouldn't have been half of the person I was if it wasn't for them. Even though I was young when my father passed, he had taught me a lot in those eight years of my life. My mother, a loving, kind, and straight-forward woman, was the flame of my candle. On my wedding night, I wanted to have one dance with the first woman I'd ever loved. Badly, I wanted to hear them say how much they loved NaTashia and how proud they were of us. Since I couldn't hear those words out of their mouths, I had to find solace in knowing I did right by them as their son and as a person.

"So, Santana's family left with her body today," NaTashia voiced, sadly, strolling into the bathroom.

Putting down my toothbrush, I walked towards my woman and replied, "I'm so sorry for the loss of your friend. Is there anything I can do to ease some of the pain?"

"No. It has to work itself out," she stated, stepping further into my arms.

"How's Cleophus taking it?"

"As best as he can."

"Do you know of any funeral arrangements?"

"No. They won't give us any closure."

"You will have to find closure in knowing how much she adored you and enjoyed being around you."

"What did he do to make them act this way?" she inquired.

" In their eyes, Cleophus ruined their daughter's dream of being all that she could be. Her parents were pissed. They didn't see their daughter with a drug dealer, and they didn't mind expressing their feelings openly. Cleophus and Santana met during her senior year at Alabama State University. They didn't start dating until she graduated. Upon graduating from college, Santana was supposed to have returned to her hometown, Chicago. She couldn't leave that fool alone, so she stayed. He didn't want her to work; thus, she didn't. Whatever she wanted, he provided without a simple thought."

While we talked about Santana and Cleophus, we hopped in the shower and quickly cleaned our bodies. Halfway through our quick shower, all of NaTashia's questions about Santana and Cleophus had been answered, which allowed for a new topic to surface. Honestly, I was thankful. I didn't want to see Nana down on the day all should be merry.

Once her laughter filled the bathroom, I knew all would be well for the rest of the day. Upon drying off and putting on Christmas lounging pajamas, we skipped into the front room with a smile on our faces. Our kids jumped up and down before running towards the packed Christmas tree. We greeted Auntie Marilyn as it seemed like she had been hit by an 18-wheeler. Her naturally long hair was a mess on top of her head. The expression on her face informed me she was wasted. She had the time of her life last night until the early morning.

Smiling, NaTashia glared at me, and lowly said, "So, this is what you were really doing for an hour and a half after ... um ... our intimate time?"

"Some like that." I smiled as I placed a kiss on her forehead.

"Auntie Marilyn told me about the gifts you purchased for us every year. I wondered where you could've put them."

"In the attic."

Oddly, Angel and Maxon shrieked in unison, "What am I supposed to do with this baby toy?"

Chuckling, I said, "Nothing now. I had purchased quite a few things for y'all over the years. Some of them are not age-appropriate. So, we are going to give them to other age-appropriate kids. Cool?"

"Super cool," Maxon stated as he placed an infant toy on the ground.

It took thirty minutes for the kids to open their gifts before I blindfolded Nana and moved her towards the front door. As I slowly and carefully opened the rectangular object, I gently pushed her closer towards the screen door.

"What do you have up your sleeves now, Fabian?" she happily stated.

Before I could open my mouth, the kids hollered, "Holy cow!"

"What is it?" NaTashia anxiously asked as Auntie Marilyn laughed before placing her forefinger to her lips.

"Keep your eyes closed until I say open them."

"Okay," NaTashia voiced, fidgeting.

I removed the blindfold from her face and said, "Open your eyes, Nana."

Busting out laughing, she said, "Really, Fabian? Like really?"

"Yeah, why not. You have always been fascinated with old school, tricked out cars, so I got you one. Everything in it is custom; since you don't like to drive fast, I didn't have the motor supped up. You can hop in something modern, more family-like on days you don't want to drive the old school car. I pegged you as a car chick since you never drive my SUV. So, I hope you like the color of your Hyundai Elantra." I smiled, handing her two sets of keys.

"I love it. I love both of them, especially that SS Monte Carlo. Oh, that matte army green is hitting with the gold rims. You did put me some speakers in the back, right?" she smiled, glaring up at me.

Nodding, I replied, "Now, you know I did that."

"Now um, tell me, why are there horses and a carriage stopping in front of our house??" she spoke as the kids went crazy, hooting and hollering.

"I always wanted to stroll around the city or neighborhood in a horse and carriage with my family. So, I asked Mr. John, our neighbor to the right, to help me out."

"Did you have it in mind for us to be dressed up or in our Christmas lounging wear?" Nana inquired.

"Since we have on matching Christmas clothing, I saw we go as we are," I replied as the children agreed.

"Then, it's a go," my wife voiced as I saw Mr. John walking into our yard.

Opening the door, I merrily voiced, "Merry Christmas, Mr. John."

"Merry Christmas, Fabian. Y'all ready??" the elderly man inquired with a smile on his face.

"Yes, we are."

"All right then," he quickly spoke as our female neighbor across the street called his name.

"When y'all are ready, hop in the carriage. I'll be there soon after," he spoke, walking towards the yapping woman.

"Yes, sir," I replied before closing the screen door.

As I closed the screen door, NaTashia and the kids were dressed entirely with huge smiles on their faces.

"Baby, here you go," Nana beautifully voiced stated as she handed me a jacket and a pair of boots, the same as theirs.

Loudly and happily, I said, "Auntie Marilyn, please fix your hair and put on the boots and jacket that I horribly wrapped under the tree. They are closest to the sofa. Don't judge my wrapping skills; you know I suck at it. Before you say one smart thing, yes, the ugly wrapping gifts are yours, and no, you can't open them yet. You gotta wait until we get back. Deal?"

"Deal," she laughed.

Five minutes later, we climbed in the carriage. The children and Auntie Marilyn sat in the second row, and my wife and I sat in the last row.

"Are y'all ready?" Mr. John asked, looking back at us.

"Yes," we loudly replied.

As the horses moved away from the curb, I loved seeing the smiles on my family's faces. I loved feeling the wind whipping across my face as the horses trotted down the road. The laughter from the kids overwhelmed me as they hollered this was the best Christmas they've had yet. My heart was content and filled with nothing but love and peace. My life was complete, and I couldn't wish or pray for anything more. I really had it all.

Sighing peacefully, my wife snuggled in the crook of my arm and pointed upward. I looked into the sky. It was the most beautiful blue I had seen. The clouds were minimal.

"Not there, silly," she laughed.

"You pointed upwards, woman," I chuckled.

"Look closely," she cooed as she brought attention to her head.

"Oh!" I laughed and shook my head.

NaTashia had pinned her hair into a messy bun. At the tip of the bun were several mistletoes.

"That's why you had the hood over your head. You sneaky little woman you," I voiced as I placed the hood over her head and planted my hand on her cheek.

"To a wonderful life, filled with love, patience, kindness, plenty of nasty sex, laughter, and great memories," she sincerely voiced, searching my eyes.

"To a wonderful life, filled with love, patience, kindness, plenty of nasty sex, laughter, and great memories," I recited before I parted my wife's lips with my tongue.

Epilogue

NaTashia

Friday, December 4th, 2020

Pigeon Forge, Tennessee

"This shit is for the birds!" Monique yelled as sweat poured down her face.

"Keep calm, sister. Just breathe like we've practiced," I stated, feeling nauseous.

"It's easy for you to say that you aren't the one laying here with an entire baby ready to bust through your coochie. I've been in labor since we got here. This isn't how I imagined our week up here. Why is she coming a week early?" she whined.

Smiling, I said, "Two months ago, I was in your position, just not this long of labor. She's coming early because she's ready to meet her parents, especially the one who swears he can sing."

A contraction took my sister's focus as the midwife was coaching her through it. June Bug sauntered in the room, looking pale and scared. The poor soul wasn't prepared for the arrival of their daughter. Just like I wasn't ready to find them fucking senselessly on our family trip at the beginning of March. From that day forward, they were inseparable. June Bug and Monique made a beautiful couple; they were perfect for each other.

Not far behind his friend, Fabian softly said, "Aye, baby, our little one is hungry. Care to share a titty with her?"

The headstrong midwife, a calming down Monique, and a pale-ish June Bug laughed at my husband's choice of words to breastfeed our daughter, Fabianna Chloe Wells.

As I stood, I carefully nodded. I didn't make it far before I cupped my mouth and ran past my husband and daughter.

"You good?" he asked worriedly, walking behind me.

I gave him a thumb's up before I dashed into the bathroom. I barely lifted the toilet before the remnants in my stomach found the cleaned bottom of the toilet. It seemed as if I was never going to stop puking. I hated the entire process of vomit leaving my body.

As I threw up, from behind me, Rebecca said, "Seems like you are pregnant. You barely eat. You do drink plenty of liquids. Now, you are vomiting. It's been like that for a little over two weeks. So, I took the liberty of purchasing a pregnancy test."

Upon my body releasing the chunks of nastiness, I disposed of the mess before cleaning my mouth. Fabiana softly wailed; I had to hurry. She was an impatient little, greedy one.

Exiting the bathroom, I glared into my husband's face as he handed me Fabiana and her blanket.

"You sure you are all right?" he asked, rubbing my stomach.

"For the time being, yes," I replied as I situated our little one so she could receive my breast milk.

"Have you talked to Cleophus?"

"No. Have you?"

"Yeah."

"When will he arrive up here?" I inquired, glaring into his eyes.

"He's not coming. He took Bailey and the kids to Busch Gardens, Virginia."

"Oh, wow. So, he's decided to be in a relationship with Bailey?"

"I think so. He's been spending a lot of time with her and the kids. After Santana passed, he couldn't get his mind right. It was Bailey who pulled him through, not the kids, not June Bug, or me. Honestly, I can say I'm glad she was there for him in a way we couldn't be. I'm proud she was able to get him to see life again. He sees it differently. Trust me when I say that fool is still a fool, but he isn't the same childish and don't think things through fool. He's finally grown into what a man supposed to be."

Proud to hear good things about my uncle, I still worried that he wasn't in his right frame of mind. If he didn't see the goodness in Bailey before, why see it now. Just that quickly, at the mention of her name, all sorts of negative things consumed my mind.

"Whatever you are thinking, cease it, Nana. Bailey isn't going to hurt your uncle or has done anything to make him be with her. He's doing everything on his own. Keep in mind, I know Bailey well enough to say she has my partner's best interest at heart."

Clearing my throat, I replied, "If that's so, why did she bring her ass down here last year ...

knowing damn well he had someone he truly loved. Honestly, I believed Santana would've never flown off the handle like that if Bailey didn't pop off at the mouth. I'm very sure June Bug wouldn't have shot her, which was a part of the reason she died. So, whatever you know doesn't compare to how I feel."

Seeing where our conversation was going, for the two-hundredth time, I held up my hands and said, "I know when I'm going to lose a battle. Therefore, we will cease talks about that conversation and enjoy what's in front of us. Okay?"

Deeply inhaling, I nodded and said, "Okay."

As Fabian walked beside me into the front room of the large cabin, which was filled with laughter, my thoughts of last year's situation was no longer an issue. My heart lit up like a Christmas tree upon seeing everyone spreading love, holiday cheer, and warmth.

There had been a tremendous change in our lives. Last Christmas, Liddia and I came up with the best proposal for our children. That they would spend every holiday together. If we could work out the weekend schedules of them being together, it would be a plus. On New Year's Eve last year, Liddia and I decided that each month's second and fourth weekend would be dedicated to the kids spending time with each other.

Standing, Liddia happily said, "So, I've gotten to know everyone in this room. I'm not going to lie; at first, I was skeptical about my children and me being around you guys. I humbly apologize for my thinking. I have never witnessed a more knit tight, loving, happy, and fun family. I have never known such joy until I've became more acquainted with everyone. Oh, the love you all spread is amazing. I couldn't think of better people to be around during any day of the week. So thoughtful, kind, and generous with your love. None of this wouldn't have been possible without you, NaTashia. I thank you for everything. You've allowed me to see what happiness, peace, love, and joy really is. Mother to mother, woman to woman, and sister-in-law to sister-in-law, I need to say, I truly honor, respect, and love you."

Walking in from the side porch of the large cabin, my handsome and tall brother, Orthello smiled, "Um, bae, it's y'all. We don't do that 'you all' talk."

As I was confused at my brother's comment, Auntie Marilyn hollered, "Gotdamn it, I knew it!

I knew it! Vincent, Danya, Sasha, run me my money now!"

While my siblings hopped up, hooting and hollering, they dug in their pockets, retrieving a wad of cash. I was still lost.

"What? What is going on?" I asked, dumbfounded.

Laughing, Fabian said, "You still don't pay attention to detail."

It seemed as if a lightning rod had struck me; with bucked eyes, I said, "Shit. Oh wow. You did say sister-in-law to sister-in-law. When did this happen? Now, you and I, Liddia, need to follow suit into Fabian's and my room soon as the little one is fed. I have some catching up to do."

"Fourth of July weekend," she happily stated as my brother slid beside her, placing a kiss on her neck and a hand on her belly.

The house erupted in applause as June Bug's weakly yelled, "Ma'Riyah has made her entrance."

Before I could rejoice in happiness and hug him, he passed out.

"That damn boy can't stomach shit," Auntie Marilyn laughed as Vincent held tightly onto our friend.

Shortly afterward, we welcomed the news of Ma'Riyah arriving and Orthello and Liddia bringing a new life into our family.

"I think you need to take the test now. I placed the test on your bed. I'll hold little juicy," Rebecca whispered in my ear as one hell of a celebration took place.

While nodding my head, I handed Fabiana to her great-aunt/step-grandmother. As Fabian talked to the fellas, I quickly and politely asked him to step into the bedroom with me. Instantly, his face lit up.

"Not for that, sir," I giggled, grabbing his hand before whisking him away.

As we sauntered down the hallway, the midwife spoke happily, "Both are ready to have visitors."

Nodding, I replied, "Perfect. We will be in shortly."

Dashing into our room, I rapidly snatched up the pregnancy test and said, "To the bathroom, we go."

"What? Hold up, you don't think I got you knocked up again, do you?" he asked with a crooked smile.

Rolling my eyes, I said, "It's not like we use condoms, sir. No bleeding and deep strokes took place soon as Fabiana turned four weeks, sir."

In his fake British accent, Fabian goofily spoke, "After you, milady."

Laughing, I walked off on the man who was obsessed with historical British royalty and their customs.

Once in the bathroom, it took me a while to pee. Proud of the moment it started to flow, Fabian stood in front of me, cheering as he never took his eyes away from the scene in front of him. Laughing at him, piss splashed onto my fingers.

"Pissy hand, woman," he chuckled.

"Shut up," I told him as I placed the test on the sink's counter.

After cleaning myself and washing my hands, we patiently waited for the results. While we did so, I was up against the wall as my husband's hands ravished my body and his tongue explored my mouth.

"Think we can sneak away to our room for a quick session in 'The Quiet Game'," he breathed against my lips as he rubbed my fat girl.

"Nope. Too much going on. I think it would be best to wait until everyone settles down for the night; we can participate in some nasty sex in the car. What do you say about that?"

"With handcuffs and whip cream?" he questioned, eyebrow raised.

"Don't forget the ankle restraints," I spoke provocatively as I pressed my hands against his chest, signaling for him to step back.

"Oouu, I like when you don't want to move and eager to take all this dick and mouth," he replied as I planted my eyes on the test.

With a blank facial expression, I held up the pregnancy test. A sad look was on his face as he said, "Well damn. I guess we will try extra hard, huh?"

Shaking my head and laughing, I asked, "You didn't look at the damn thing."

"For what? Your face told it all."

"Look at it!" I laughed.

Sighing deeply, he did as I asked of him. That sad face turned into a happy one. Instantly, he started shouted, "That's what the fuck I'm talking 'bout! Get in there, get in there!"

"I told you I have a mean Poker face when I want to use it," I voiced, wrapping my hand around his neck.

"Yes, you do," he replied, picking me up and continuing, "Think it's a boy this time?"

"Probably so because I was at that dick, morning, noon, and night. All outside on top of the cars, I was riding that thang and making your toes curl," I voiced, pussy popping.

Opening the door, Fabian laughed. While walking down the hallway, like the boss man he was, Fabian flipped the kitchen lights several times.

The noise simmered down low enough for him to shout, "This protein shake be workinggg!"

"Boy!" Danya choked as she spat her beverage all over Vincent.

"I swear before God, you have a way with words, fool! Congratulations, nigga!" Orthello laughed before everyone caught on to what was being announced.

Several rounds of congratulations sounded off for Monique, Liddia, and myself.

"What is all this noise for?" Monique asked, standing a few inches from behind us.

"You've had a successful delivery. Liddia and Orthello are having a baby, and Fabian swelled my uterus up again." I smiled, climbing off Fabian.

Holding onto the wall, Monique loudly and excitedly said, "Sasha, Danya, and Vincent, I told y'all our brother and Liddia were too friendly!

Y'all can run me my motherfuckin' coins! You can pay me in nickels and dimes! I don't give a damn, but hannit hea!"

While everyone laughed at my silly sister, Auntie Marilyn told everyone why she suspected what was going on with Orthello and Liddia.

While that conversation was going on, my sister hugged me and said, "Congratulations. You are finally getting everything you deserved. I'm so happy and proud of you."

Placing a kiss on her cheek, I replied, "As I am happy and proud of you and June Bug. Y'all make a beautiful couple and family."

While our family sang urban Christmas songs and the children occupied the game room, Fabian and I were in a world of our own.

Snatching me close to him, my doting husband planted many kisses on my forehead, nose, and lips while rubbing my belly. As we glared into each other's eyes, he lovingly said, "You are my everything and always will be. Every day of our lives, we will be merry. We will be the glue to our family. We will continue being role models and show them what love really looks and feel like. If you are tired of hearing me say 'thank you for giving me life', oh well, because not only have you blessed me … you've blessed a woman who had stripped you and our kids from what they knew. I love you so much for being you. Damn, I love this life with you, Nana."

Placing my hands on the sides of his face, I searched his eyes and sincerely spoke, "Fabian, you are always saying I saved you, but it was you who saved me. In the beginning, I was hell-bent on not trusting myself or another man. It was you who breathed *real* life into me. It was you pushing me off the swing, placing me in your life forever. It was you always thinking of me, first. It was you completing dangerous acts in the streets to make sure I never went without. You've saved me more times than I can count or probably don't know of. So, instead of you telling me thank you, it's me that must tell you … thank you for being my best friend. Thank you for loving me, unconditionally. Thank you for still keeping me close to your heart during the years I was away. I love you, and I can't wait to have one or two more pregnancies after this one. Like we said many years before, 'it'll always be us'. I love you so much, baby."

"As I love you, NaTashia Wells," he breathed against my lips before parting them with his liquor-filled, thick and long tongue.

About the Novelist

TN Jones

TN Jones was born and raised in Alabama, which she resides in her home state with her daughter. Growing up, TN Jones always had a passion for reading and writing, which led her to create short stories during her teenage years.

In 2015, TN Jones began working on her first book, *Disloyal: Revenge of a Broken Heart*, which was previously titled, *Passionate Betrayals*.

TN Jones writes in the following Urban/Interracial fictional genres: Women's/Romance, Chick Lit, Mystery/Suspense, Dark Erotica/Erotica, and Paranormal.

Published novels by TN Jones: *By Any Means: Going Against the Grain 1-2, The Sins of Love: Finessing the Enemies 1-3, Caught Up In a D-Boy's Illest Love 1-3, Choosing To Love A Lady Thug 1-4, Is This Your Man, Sis: Side Piece Chronicles, Just You and Me: A Magical Love Story, Jonesin' For A Boss Chick: A Montgomery Love Story, That Young Hood Love 1-2, Give Me What I Want, If My Walls Could Talk, A Sucka for a Thug's Love, Her Mattress Buddy, Chocolate Enchantress, I Now Pronounce You Mr. and Mrs. Thug 1-3, Disloyal 1-3, Hood Lovin': Santa Sent me a Hoodlum, Santa Sauce: A Kinky Christmas Tale, Baby Be Mine: Lovin' on My Hoodlum, I'm All Yours, Do Me Baby*, and *Barcoded Pu**y.*

Collaboration novel: Dating a Female Goon with Ms. Biggz (paperback purchase can be made via authors)

Anthologies: Big Girls Love Dope Boys Too (Genesys & Adonis)

Re-releases: If You'll Give Me Your Heart *1-3.* Dates TBA.

Upcoming novels by TN Jones: Rock Me Tonight: A Nympho's Tale & Impatient.

Thank you for reading the Christmas-themed standalone novel, *Under the Mistletoe: Love from a Hood Pharmacist.* Please leave an honest review under the book title on Amazon and Goodreads.

For future book details, please visit any of the links below:

Amazon Author page: https://www.amazon.com/tnjones666

Black Junction: https://blackjunction.com/TNJones

Black Junction Fan Page: https://blackjunction.com/novelisttnjones

Bookfam (formerly called Bookstagram): @Novelist TN Jones

Facebook: https://www.facebook.com/novelisttnjones/

Goodreads: https://www.goodreads.com/author/show/14 918893.TN_Jones:

Goodreads Creative Writing Blog: bit.ly/37Sz5Po

Pinterest: https://www.pinterest.com/tnjones666/

Twitter: https://twitter.com/TNJones666
Wattpad: @TNJones6

You are welcome to *email* her:
tnjones666@gmail.com
Chat with her daily in the *Facebook* group: *It's Just Me...TN Jones*
https://www.facebook.com/groups/itsjustmet njones/

Text TN Jones to 844-741-0661 to join her text VIP Club!

Did You *Enjoy* This Book?

Leaving an honest review is beneficial for me as an author. It is one of the most potent tools used as I seek attention for my books. Receiving feedback from readers will increase my chances of reaching other readers who haven't read a book me. Word of mouth is a great way to spread the news of a book that you've enjoyed.

With that being said, once you reach this page, please scroll to the review section and leave an honest review. Be sure to click the boxes for Goodreads and Amazon. As always, thank you for taking a chance on allowing me to provide you with quality entertainment.

Peace and Blessings, Loves!

Sneak Peek – January 1ˢᵗ 2021

"Great sex is a natural drug,"– Toba Beta

Chapter One
Aydin Marshall

The past three months had been hard for me. I had to get away from the sadness. I needed to breathe before shit really sunk in for me. My mind needed to be fearless and less worried, or I would run off the deep end. I needed to have fun and smile until my jaws hurt. I needed my life to be the way it was before my father became gravely ill. Just for the night, I needed normalcy. Simply put, I needed just a little bit of peace.

"Too much, bitch I thank I'm too much," my best friend, Arcadia Simmons, and I sang while dancing in Club Royce's chairs.

As we vibed to Ms. Shyne's "Too Much", two guys strolled towards our table. I wasn't interested; therefore, I acted like the stuck-up female many guys had called me. I didn't have time to deal with any liars and players. However, my best friend was all for the fuckery. Arcadia was in a situationship; I wouldn't dare call it a relationship. That character wasn't good enough for my girl. Time and time again, I told her to put the trash where it belonged. Since they had 'history', she acted like she couldn't toss the nigga to the next female.

"Hey, Miss Lady. Why are you sittin' ova here wit' that look on yo' face? You are too beautiful to look like that?" the unwanted male whispered into my ear.

I couldn't lie as if he didn't look good because he did. His choice of cologne was enticing. Yet, I stood firm on not wanting to be bothered. Thus, I told him a little something that had him out of my face before closing my mouth good enough.

Laughing, Arcadia tapped my wrist before pulling it towards her. When I placed my ear to her mouth, she asked, "Bitch, what you told that man to have him flying away from you?"

With a smile on my face, I glared at my best friend, leaned towards her, and said, "I told his ass I was a mental patient, and he didn't want me stalking him nor busting out his car windows and shit of that nature."

Busting out laughing, Arcadia shook her head. Sitting upright, we danced in the chair as I observed the club scene. We weren't in a hot zone; however, in the city we lived in, anything was liable to happen at any moment. To be safe and completely aware of the people surrounding us, I had to know if there was any negative tension within the club. If any foolery popped off, I wanted us out of harm's way. Seeing that the party-goers attitudes were enough for me to relax, I did so as I pulled Arcadia out of the chair. It was time for another drink, followed by dancing. After all, we did come to the club to have fun.

For an hour and a half, Arcadia and I danced like we were in our twenties. Guys tried their best to dance with us, but we shooed them away. The dance floor's vibe became different upon a few females evilly eyeing us and talking amongst themselves. Feeling uncomfortable, I brought the news to Arcadia. That heifer looked at me and rolled her eyes. Instantly, I laughed and continued grooving to a song.

After a few rounds of dancing with my bestie, I grew tired of dancing. As we pranced off the dance floor, the envious females had an ugly expression written on their faces while they watched us walk away. Close to our table, a familiar scent filled my nose. Immediately, I stopped walking and began to look around me.

He's not here, Aydin. He's not the only one who where's that cologne, Aydin. Chill out, I thought as I turned forward, facing the one person I didn't want to see.

Shit. The time hasn't come yet. No. No. No, I thought as Luca held a grim expression on his handsome face as he pulled me close to him.

While searching his dark-brown, medium eyes, I started to tremble.

Bringing his mouth to my ear, Luca huskily said, "It's time to go."

Looking into his eyes, I rapidly shook my head.

"It's non-negotiable, Aydin. I've been calling you for the past two hours. Why in the hell are you in a club anyway? You said you were going over to Arcadia's house for a while to prepare yourself. The time has arrived."

Feeling every cell in my body divide and separate, I felt as if I was going to explode before disappearing into thin air. The air in my chest became far and few. My eyes scurried as I tried to keep the tears away. I clenched my jaws tightly to keep my lips from quivering. As many happy and treasured images of my parents and me surfaced, my knees buckled.

Luca caught me before I dropped to the ground. Picking me up, Luca sincerely said, "I'm so sorry, Aydin. I'm so sorry you have to deal with this."

As he carried me out of the club, Arcadia wasn't far behind with a sad expression on her beautiful, light-skinned face.

"Where did you park?" Luca asked, walking towards the parking lot.

I couldn't speak; therefore, Arcadia answered, "She rode with me."

"Okay. Where's your car?" Luca asked, looking at my best friend.

"Right there," she replied.

"All right. I'm going to stand here and watch you get into your car safely. I will take Aydin to her parents' house."

Before Arcadia could respond, I said, "No, I want to go to my apartment. I will face the music tomorrow."

Sternly, Luca said, "No, you will go to your parents' house. You and your mother need each other right now."

Through clenched teeth, I sternly spoke, "I don't want to go there. I want to go to my place and fuck on every piece of furniture. I want dick deep down my throat as I squeeze on balls. I want my pussy sore by the time I wake up tomorrow. I want to feel good, not pain, because of my father's death. I want to have my hair pulled while I'm getting fucked from the back. I want my tongue deep in a motherfucker's mouth to the point he's damn near choking. So, Luca James, what you are going to do is take me the fuck home because I'm not ready to mourn the death of my father. I'm ... simply ... not ... fucking ... ready."

While glaring at me, I saw the sadness in his eyes. Nodding, Luca placed his eyes on Arcadia and said, "She'll be fine. She'll call you in the morning. Be safe on your trip home."

Oddly, Arcadia replied, "Okay."

Before walking away, my best friend placed a kiss on my forehead and sincerely said, "I'm so sorry for the loss of your father. I will give you and Mrs. Angie some time. I'll see you in the morning. I love you, Aydin."

"I love you too," I softly replied.

As Luca traveled towards his vehicle, he didn't say a word. I was sure he was lost in his thoughts. After all, his best friend had passed away.

Realizing I was selfish, I gently said, "I'm sorry for the loss of your best friend."

While walking, Luca nodded and pressed the unlock button on the key fob. After placing me in the passenger seat, Luca kneeled, grabbed my hand, and said, "You know you just pissed me off, right?"

Nodding, I lowly voiced, "Yeah, I know."

Clearing his throat, he rubbed his beard and replied, "I'm going to give you exactly what you want, but it will be after we've grieved your father. Do I make myself clear?"

Shaking my head, I responded smartly, "You know that is not a good move. Either give me what I want now or don't give it to me at all."

Growling, Luca said, "I said what the fuck I said, Aydin Marshall. You are going to handle his passing the right way. I will not allow his death to be the ruin of you. You have come a long way. You will continue to be on the straight and narrow path."

Gazing into his eyes, I slowly spoke through clenched teeth, "You are going to fuck me, and you are going to do it right ... as you always have. You are going to put me in my place so I can bury my father without any regrets. Do ... I ... make ... myself ... fucking clear? I'm sure you don't want another motherfucker playing in this juicy pussy, huh?"

I bet he's going to give me what the fuck I want now. He hates to be threatened, I thought as Luca sinisterly chuckled and put the seatbelt around my frame.

I watched the handsome, older man walk in front of his new model, black Mercedes, shaking his head. Before he arrived at the driver's door, I leaned over and opened the door for the man who aided me in my nymphomaniac ways. While sitting, Luca exhaled and inhaled several times. His breathing was heavy; he was on the verge of going off on me. Placing the key in the ignition, Luca looked at me with the sexiest and sternest expression on his face, which turned me on.

He knows what I need to have a calm mind, and there is no doubt he's going to give me just that, I thought cooing.

Luca lost his cool and said, "You really need to chill out, Aydin. I need you to cry. I need you to feel the pain, not run from it."

Rolling my eyes, I shook my head and said, "I'm not ready to feel that type of pain, Luca. I'm sure you understand."

As he started the engine, he loudly spat, "No, I don't understand, and I never will."

"And that's the difference between you and me."

Skirting away from the club's parking lot, Luca didn't say a word to me as I pondered whether he was really taking me to my parents' home.

Tired of the quietness, I asked, "Where are you taking me?"

"To your parents' home like I said."

"I was clear where I wanted to go and what I wanted to do, Luca," I voiced, glaring at him.

Through clenched teeth, he said, "As I was clear about what I said. I don't like repeating myself, Aydin, you know this. Don't start any shit, and it won't be any."

With a disappointed facial expression, I aggressively nodded and folded my arms. Doing what I knew to do best, I pouted and huffed; I was beyond pissed I wouldn't receive the one thing that would help me before I officially stepped into grieving my father.

Luca James was the type of man who reeked of control and lived on protecting those he cared about; what he said goes. I knew when to push him and when to back off. However, I knew he was weak for my actions. If I didn't want to go to my parents' house, the best thing to do was to show him why he shouldn't take me until I was ready.

I be damned if I go to my parents' house tonight. After satisfying the need to feel something other than the turmoil of my father's passing, I will surface, I thought as I quickly and roughly unbuckled his belt and unzipped his pants.

"What are you doing?" he inquired, looking at me briefly.

Holding his perfect lengthy and heavenly girth dick in my hand, I replied, "Doing what you are not willing to ... initiate some shit."

While I began to slowly massage his pussy pleaser, I removed my seatbelt.

Trying to remove my hand, Luca moaned, "No, we are not going to do this."

Gripping his dick tighter, I yelled, "Stop fighting me! You've never fought me before, and you will not start now!"

In a calm yet stern manner, Luca voiced, "Who are you yelling at, Aydin?"

Releasing his member, I replied smartly, "You."

Chuckling, Luca nodded, pressed the hazard button, and pulled onto the side of the road. Glaring at him, I wondered what words of encouragement were going to come out of his mouth.

As he unbuckled his seat belt, Luca said, "You are one spoiled ass female. You can't get your way every time you pout or yell. You do know that, right?"

Not wanting to hear his unnecessary speech, I sighed sharply and looked out of the window. The neighborhood he had pulled over in, I wouldn't have done it. We were in the middle of the hood, the part that had bandos and plenty of crackheads.

"Look at me when I'm talking to you, Aydin!" he shouted, startling me.

I have officially pissed him off, and I don't give a damn. He should've given me what I asked for, I thought as I placed my eyes on him.

Luca's expression had the seat of my thongs wet. He was angry yet so damn fine. I wanted to suck his lips off his face while rubbing his bald, shiny head.

"Why must you make shit so hard for me?" he softly asked, grabbing my hand.

With an attitude, I replied, "If I make things that hard for you, why continue dealing with me? Let me go, and I'll be someone else's problem."

For God knows how long, Luca glared at me and growled. I was officially in trouble with the man I had been secretly fucking, off and on, since I was eighteen.

"Take off your fucking clothes, Aydin," he spoke through clenched teeth.

"You have to be out of your damn mind if you think I'm going to get naked in this car. Look where we are, Luca," I stated, pointing out of the window.

"I'm not about to play this game with your ass!" he responded, reclining his seat.

"Take me to my parents' house, Luca," I voiced, folding my arms and looking straight ahead.

"I said come out of your fucking clothes, Aydin!"

"And I said take me to my parents' hou—"

"You going to turn me into a being I left behind a long time ago," he voiced as he began to undress me.

By the time he finished fussing at me, he was placing me on his face. I was one paranoid female as I nervously looked around. I was sure someone was going to approach the car.

Nervously, I said, "We are not about to do this here, Luca."

With my legs dangling off the driver's seat, Luca glared into my face and said, "You ... fuck ... you are ... fuck it."

One flick from his tongue sent chills running through my body as my limbs became weak. Enveloping his mouth around my precious kitty, I began not to care about where we were or what could happen if the wrong person approached his vehicle.

"Mhm," Luca voiced as his tongue made circles around the opening of my pussy. Shortly afterward, he devoured my hairless girl. He took his time tasting dipping his tongue inside of my pretty girl before latching onto my pink bud.

"Shii," I cooed as my body shook uncontrollably.

Ring. Ring. Ring.

As Luca's phone rang, he slipped a finger into my asshole, driving me insane.

"Lucaaa!" I squealed, gripping the seat and fucking his tongue.

Wonderful pussy eating noises escaped his mouth. A moment or two later, I came so hard my body locked. While removing his finger out of my asshole, Luca slipped two fingers into my coochie and sucked on my pink bud, aggressively and passionately.

"This is all you had to do from the beginning, Luca. Pacify me," I groaned, holding tightly to the back of his head.

Upon being satisfied with my juices filling him up, Luca placed my shaking body in the passenger seat. After sliding the seat back as far as it could go, Luca's husky and long body found its way in between my legs. While I gazed at the handsome man with teary eyes, he glared at me with a blank expression.

With his dick in his hand, Luca French-kissed my pussy once more before placing his beast inside of my leaky core. On the side of the road, in the gotdamn hood, Luca rocked me until tears streamed down my face. There wasn't any music playing, just the sounds of moaning, groaning, and our bodies connecting beautifully and roughly. There wasn't anything to say. There wasn't any need for 'I love you's', "I need you's', or anything of that nature. We knew how we felt about each other. We had been expressing it for years, even when I broke things off.

After placing his hand around my neck and applying light pressure, Luca planted his nose on mine and said, "After I'm done speaking, you will learn to watch your damn mouth. You will learn that I'm nothing to play with when it comes down to you. Do I make myself clear?"

While thrusting my pretty girl on his pole, I nodded and cooed, "Yesss."

"Good. You said you wanted your hair pulled and dicked down until you hurt, right?"

As our slow thrusts got the best of me, I weakly replied, "I don't know about the dicking me down until I hurt."

With a wicked smile, he replied, "I do."

Oh shit, I thought as he placed my legs behind my head, leaned backward, and chuckled.

I'm fucked, I thought as he sucked on my toes.

"Luca," I sexily moaned.

"Nawl, it's too late to get some act right. Just know you brought this on yourself, Chocolate Drop."

Fu—, "Luc—"

My breathing and thoughts were taken away as he pummeled my pussy. With every fifth deep stroke, Luca popped my thighs. Badly, I wanted to apologize for my behavior; however, the way he was delivering the dick, I couldn't say a single word.

"You think you can talk to me like I'm a little ass nigga. Aydin, you got shit fucked up. You keep forgetting who the fuck I really am to you. I'm not a simp ass nigga. I ... am ... that ... motherfucking ... nigga!" he growled, nose to nose—digging deeper into my gushy nectar.

"I'm sor—"

"I don't even want to hear it. You wanted this, so you got just what your little chocolate ass asked for and more," he hissed as my body became extremely aroused and hot.

Pinned against the seat, I became a nutty mess as I found the will to poorly call his name.

"I swore I said shut up, Aydin," he growled, smacking my thigh and applying pressure to my neck, all the while pounding out my girl.

Oh God, I thought as I enjoyed the rough sex.

A few seconds later, my eyes were bucked as my body experienced one of many back-arching orgasms.

"Yeahhh, give me all of that," Luca voiced, riding me as if I was a prized stallion.

"I love you, Luca!" I shouted as a car bypassed us. I was sure they noticed the rocking vehicle on the side of the street, but I didn't care. All I cared about was the man in between my legs, giving me exactly what I needed.

Applying more pressure to my neck, Luca glared into my eyes and said, "The next time you say some flip shit out of your mouth, I will fuck you non-stop. I won't care if your pussy is aching. I won't care if you can't speak because you've moaned, groaned, and screamed entirely too much. I won't care where we are. To be clear about this threat, if you get beside yourself, I will fuck you in your parents' house, all the while gripping your hair and ass. Trust, I will fuck you until you submit ... the right way. I will miss personal and business events just to make sure my dick is deep within your walls. Do I make myself clear, Aydin Marshall?"

I couldn't respond because I was on the verge of having another big orgasm.

Thrusting deeper, Luca spoke through clenched teeth, "I said, do I make myself clear?"

"Ahh, yes. Yes, you've made yourself clear. Baby, I swear you've made yourself clear."

"Good," he voiced before asking, "Where you want me to nut at?"

With teary eyes, I said, "In me."

"Are you sure?"

"Yes."

Removing his hand from around my neck, Luca sucked my bottom lip into his mouth before sticking his tongue into my warm, wet mouth. The passionate and beautiful lovemaking took place until his sperm was swimming inside of my lovely coochie, going to the only place it was destined to be.

As he broke our kiss, Luca rubbed the sides of my face and glared into my eyes for a while. Like always, after a heated sexual moment, Luca was in his feelings. Breathlessly and patiently, I waited for him to speak his peace as he'd done so many times before.

"I'll love you until I have no breath in my body. I'll always be here to protect and care for you. You are everything I need and want. All I see is you, Aydin. Please don't push me away. We've come too far. Hell, you've come too far. Allow me to be in your life from here on out. I don't want this ... our happiness to leave. I don't want us to be back in the same position we were in years ago. I need to be in your life, and not just for some random sexual pleasure. I'm really tired of stressing this to you. I really need you to think about it. I mean, really think about it. Okay?"

"Okay," I voiced while thinking; we can't be together, Luca. Our union will cause drama, and I'm not a drama type of woman. This will be our last time. It has to be. People will be hurt, and I don't want to hurt anyone because I'm in love with you, and I need you. That's why I broke things off between us years ago.

As he helped me put on my clothes, the silence became a bit too much for me. I didn't want to be left alone with my thoughts and the current situation between Luca and me. I thought having sex would alleviate the way I felt, at least for a little while, but it didn't. Having sex with Luca only brought more pain my way. I disliked knowing I couldn't have him the way I needed to.

"Talk to me, Aydin."

"There isn't anything to say."

"What's wrong?"

"Nothing."

"Stop lying to me. Tell me what's on your mind?" Luca questioned before climbing into the driver's seat and fixing his clothes.

Sighing deeply, I said, "We can't be together. I'm sorry, Luca, but I can't hurt those I've spent all of my life around. I'm sorry, but this is our last time being around the other without an ounce of clothes on. Don't debate me on this; just take me to my parents' house in silence, please. Honestly, it was a mistake for me to open my legs to you after all of these years, especially after I vowed never to be with you again. If you didn't hear me the first time, Luca James, I'm going to repeat it... it's over and for good this time."

Made in the USA
Columbia, SC
27 June 2021